TIED TO THE ALIEN TYRANT

A CRASHLAND CASTAWAY ROMANCE

LESLIE CHASE
STARR HUNTRESS

Tied to the Alien Tyrant

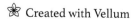 Created with Vellum

ABOUT CRASHLAND

Tied to the Alien Tyrant is the third book in the CRASHLAND CASTAWAY ROMANCES, a trilogy of books that follows on from the CRASHLAND COLONY ROMANCES. You don't need to read Colony to follow the Castaway books, but if you want to find out more about how humans came to crash on this planet, that's where to look!

Crashland Colony Romances

On the trip to Arcadia Colony carrying a cargo of human colonists in suspended animation, the *Wandering Star* is attacked by Prytheen pirates. The muscular blue alien warriors want the terraforming equipment aboard and will stop at nothing to get it.

Auric, a Prytheen alpha, decides to protect the humans, racing ahead to warn them. And when he arrives, he recognizes the ship's engineer Tamara as his fated mate.

In a desperate attempt to save the colonists, Tamara jumps the ship into a forbidden system inside the Tavesh Empire. Now, stuck on an unknown planet, humans and Prytheen must work together to survive on the planet they call CRASHLAND.

Crashland Castaway Romances

The human colonists and Prytheen warriors who arrived with the *Wandering Star* aren't alone on Crashland. The native aliens, Zrin, don't know what to make of these invaders from beyond the sky. Some see the visitors as gods, some as demons. Others see a chance to change their civilization forever.

Things only get more complicated when some Zrin find their fated mates amongst the humans. Entangled in the lives of these bronze-age barbarians, the Earthwomen and their Zrin lovers must find a way to bridge the gulf between them.

1

TZARON

A strong wind from the south brought my prey's scent to me and I breathed deep, learning what I could about the strangers who'd landed on my world. Strange smells of fire and oil and unfamiliar plants carried over the purple forest to the hilltop on which I stood.

I could just about see the source of the smell — strange domes of metal and other, less familiar materials, surrounded by fields. My human prey showed their strength by farming surface crops, braving the harsh sun and dangerous animals to raise food where no Zrin would.

Powerful, stupid, or inexperienced? Or a mix of all three? The humans came from beyond the Sky, so they could have magic to face down the dangers any

Zrin would shrink from. Or they might not even know the danger they were in.

A metal bird the size of a longhouse lifted from the ground inside the settlement and flew south at a speed I found hard to believe, even after all the reports I'd heard of human magic. I smiled at the sight. So far everything was as according to my plan.

"I don't like this," Krosak said. Snarled, rather. "We are far from our territory, and we have much loot. We should return before one of the other chieftains claims power for himself."

Of course he'd waited until the very last moment to protest. My tail slashed through the air and Krosak took one look at my ssav before stepping back. I didn't need to see his to know white and gray tendrils writhed on his skin. For a warlord, my second in command was easy to frighten.

"Let anyone stupid enough to face me try," I said, grappling for control of my anger. It wasn't directed at Krosak, and there was no need to scare him. "This raid is the point of the expedition. The rest gathered supplies for the attack on the humans, remember? We've come too far now, if we turn back we'll look weak. One day's delay won't make much difference, will it?"

Krosak muttered a negative, sullen but obedient.

Let him fume as long as he obeys. Another scent on the wind, clean and natural. The scent of a gathering storm. I smiled, hands clenching into fists. Nearly time.

"Make sure the drogara are ready," I said. "And the warriors."

"Lord, we throw away good meat for bad here," Krosak said, trying again to dissuade me. I turned to frown at him — he rarely dared disagree *twice*.

And yet he continued, though his ssav was half-white with fear. "The drogara, they are excellent eating, valuable animals, good for work too. If we return with them, we will be heroes. But your plan... Lord, you risk losing them for no gain. I — I don't say this to anger you, Lord, I have your best interests at heart."

Idiot. Thinking of the next day, forgetting the next year. If I did things his way, I'd never rise beyond a petty raider-king. I took a deep breath, pushed the anger from my ssav, and tried to be charitable. Krosak *had* waited until we were alone to raise his objection, and it showed more than normal bravery to raise it at all. He was, I reminded myself, trying to help.

I clapped him on the shoulder and smiled, trying to lessen his fear of me. "Krosak, you led a band of warriors for many years, and I value your insight and advice. Still, I have my plan and I am in command here. We will do things my way and you will enjoy the results of our victory. I promise you that."

His eyes lit up and he nodded, green replacing some of the white on his scales. Easy to frighten, easy to impress — that was Krosak. A perfect second in command since he'd never dare try for my position.

"Now go, make sure everything is ready," I commanded him again. "Timing is important and we must be ready before the storm is on us."

He threw me a hurried and uncoordinated salute as he turned to run. Good: I preferred swift obedience to perfect manners.

I took one last breath of the strange-tasting air and started down the hill myself. While Krosak prepared the rest of my warband, I kept the most important and delicate task for myself.

The scouts looked up at my approach, then leaped to their feet when they realized who was coming. They were a strange breed, all slender youths, lightly equipped and wearing as little as possible. If I chose my warriors for strength, armament, or experience, I'd leave these Zrin for last.

Their other talents were much more valuable,

though. Through some secret technique they'd learned to control their ssavs, to spread the color-changing to their entire bodies. Even knowing they were there, it was hard to spot them. Those who didn't know to search for them stood no chance.

That talent made them ideal scouts, even if they sometimes looked ridiculous. Amongst the purple trees, their ssavs blended by taking on the color of lust and made them look like a squad of horny teenagers. I had trouble hiding my amusement, but I managed. I needed their skills and insulting them would do no one any good.

"Ready?" I asked. The scouts nodded in unison. They didn't like to speak or make any noise unless they had to. Nothing to give away their location on a raid.

"Remember, the curse you will feel as you approach is not real," I continued, giving them one last pep talk. Behind me, dangerously close, a voice joined mine for the next line.

"It's just a human trick," Heshra said in unison with me, and the scouts broke their silence with laughter. My teeth ground together as I struggled for control.

Anyone else would lie dead at my feet for the disrespect she showed. But Heshra knew how much

I needed her scouts and wasn't above playing to that advantage. Not that I blamed her for that — as their leader, she had to protect her people, which meant making sure I didn't take them for granted. And Heshra being Heshra, she did that by reminding me I couldn't afford to kill her.

Proving their value by taunting me was not the wisest trick, but it did the job. Even through my anger, I respected her for that. It was, at least, better than the first tactic Heshra had used.

Originally, she'd tried to seduce me, as though taking a place in my bed would protect her followers. Perhaps fortunately for us both, I felt no inclination to take her up on that offer. My ambition left me no time for non-essentials like romance. If I found my taru-ma, perhaps things would change, but I doubted it.

I swallowed my annoyance and continued. "That's right. And I trust you to deal with it."

Heshra stepped past me and nodded, a sharp up and down motion. One of her Zrin threw her a spear, which she plucked from the air before heading into the forest. Her followers grabbed their own weapons and gave me a sketch of a salute before following. I tried to keep track of them, but after two steps they'd vanished, their ssavs blending into the trees perfectly.

I had to trust they'd do their job. If not, this was about to be a very embarrassing raid.

I pushed that thought from my mind. The bones were rolling, too late to take back my bet — glorious victory or humiliating defeat, I'd face either and deal with the consequences.

Back at the main camp, I saw Krosak had done his job despite his misgivings. My warband had assembled, ready for action, and none of them were doing anything worse than snarling at each other. Ahead, the huge drogara waited, turning this way and that nervously. That had been the worst part of this plan, keeping the huge, shaggy beasts nervous but not quite frightened enough to stampede. Only a little longer.

Moving through the gathered warriors, I greeted commander after commander. Each needed their own flattery, their own moment of attention, and a warlord who forgot that brought bad blood, feuds, and chaos.

Finally, once I'd spoken to everyone, we were ready to move. Now we'd find out if the humans' magic weapons were as terrifying as I'd heard.

2

VICTORIA

*H*arsh, alien sunlight poured in past the shutters, filling the huge council chamber with bright light and dark shadows. The smell of Crashland's summer came with it, cloying and sweet, the flowers planted below the window blooming and beautiful and distracting.

Focusing on negotiations with the Joint Colony was never easy, but today I just wanted to lie down somewhere and sleep till the sun went down and the temperature dropped to something reasonable. Lifting my glass of ice water to my lips, I wished I could hold it against my face.

Never show weakness, Victoria. Mother had said it a thousand times, and to her credit, it stuck. I took a careful sip, savored the momentary chill, and set the glass down on the vast wooden table that dominated the room. The planners had meant for this room to hold delegates from all over a planet, not just the six of us gathered here, and there was space for an audience as well.

"We've talked this through a thousand times, Captain," I said. "You command the *Wandering Star,* and that's fine. That doesn't give you command over the colonists, though, and the Vale is doing its own thing."

On either side of me, Colony Representatives nodded and muttered support. The men (and it didn't help that I was the only woman on the council) were generic enough to have been clones. A touch over six foot two, blandly handsome, even their hair looked alike, despite one being blond and the other a redhead. Representatives of the Arcadia Colony Company, their records claimed they were skilled politicians. Apparently that meant not committing to anything if they could help it.

While I'd have preferred it if they'd said something out loud or made points of their own, I'd take what I could get. The colonists of the Vale elected me Speaker, making these negotiations my responsibility even if I didn't want it. For some reason, I'd assumed the other members of the council would pull their weight. That only two of them turned up at all showed me how foolish that was.

The hologram sitting across from me pulled a face. Captain Tamara Joyce had been through a lot since she brought us down on Crashland, not least of which was reclaiming the remains of the *Wandering Star* from the Prytheen pirates that crashed us here. I felt bad for adding to her troubles, but I answered to the colonists, not her.

Tamara shimmered, the holoprojection jumping and skittering a little. Our communication channels worked well under the circumstances, but it was impossible to forget that there was nearly half a planet between us. Her advisers seemed as little use as mine, and I wondered how much more we'd get done if we talked alone. Fat chance of the others allowing us to do that, though.

"We need your resources if we're ever going to get the *Wandering Star* back into space, Speaker," she tried again, starting us on the thousandth circuit around this loop of the argument. The dedication and stubbornness she'd used fighting the Prytheen was profoundly irritating to go up against myself.

"And we're willing to sell at a reasonable price," I replied. "But you don't just get them for the asking. We need parts to keep the Vale Settlement running until you have your ship back in order. Which, I'll remind you, might never happen."

I shouldn't have said it that bluntly. Perhaps if the weather had been cooler, or I'd slept better, I wouldn't have. As it was, I couldn't stop the words from escaping my throat. Captain Joyce's head snapped back as though I'd slapped her. The body language of the men flanking me shifted subtly, and I felt them distance themselves from me without moving an inch. On some level, their diplomatic training was impressive. It just wasn't *useful*.

"It will work," Tamara said. "I've modeled it carefully, and we can do this. *If* we all cooperate."

The tightness of her voice and set of her shoulders left no doubt about how much I'd pissed her off. No surprise there — she'd been the ship's engineer before her rapid and tragic elevation to the Big Chair. Of course she'd take it personally. But to her credit, she didn't lash out.

"Maybe," I conceded. "I don't doubt the theory, just the practicalities of getting the resources you need. In the meantime, we'll be working for—"

A low rumble shook the ground, cutting me off, and I froze. The Vale wasn't prone to earthquakes, and I had no experience of them. A vague memory told me to get into the doorway, or to hide under the table, or *something,* but all I could do was watch my glass vibrate its way to the table's edge. It paused for a moment and then leaped off as though pushed by some invisible cat. The crash of it shattering on the floor snapped me back to myself.

"Vassily, *what the fuck?*" My hologram companion could have relayed my words easily. There was no need to raise my voice to speak to my assistant, but some occasions called for shouting and this qualified.

Vassily slid the door open, his face pale as bone. Tall, lean, wearing a suit despite the heat, he was a younger, slighter version of the Representatives, and usually shared their air of smug superiority. Now, his arrogant smile hid behind a nervous grin and his piercing eyes scanned a report his hologram kestrel projected in front of him.

"A stampede," he answered, pulling a face of distaste that would have made me laugh under other circumstances. So fastidious, he looked as though he'd bitten into a lemon rather than reporting a disaster. "Bigfurs."

I winced and gestured for him to continue.

"Something went wrong on the north slope defenses. It didn't show on diagnostics, no idea how long it's been a problem. The techs only found out when the stampeding bigfurs pushed through."

Of course there's a stampede. Of course it's bigfurs. I resisted the urge to punch the table, scream, or really indulge myself and do both. Morale was everything in a settlement this small, and letting something like this happen... well, that would hurt. *Look on the bright side. Maybe it would get me out of leading this mess of a settlement and someone else can have the honor of telling Captain Joyce 'no' every two weeks.*

My attempt at humor didn't even make me smile. If I lost the Speaker's chair, someone else would take it, and none of the candidates for the post were comforting. Vassily was the best of the bunch, and his leadership had never impressed me. Efficient, clever, but not assertive enough. He needed a guiding hand, though he'd never admit it.

I glanced left at the most likely candidate, Vincent Powry. He lacked the emotions needed to look horrified at the news, his thin, pinched face remained still while his cold mind thought through his response. A response that would benefit Representative Powry.

No time to wait for him to work out what his best move was, not with a herd of animals larger than any elephants stampeding toward the settlement. The other Representatives called up their own companion AIs and looked at the reports with wide eyes. No time for that, either.

"Emergency. Got to go," I told Captain Joyce, who nodded and closed the connection without a word. Some might have called that rude, but I was grateful she hadn't wasted time on goodbyes. Perhaps alone of all the people on Crashland, she understood the pressure I had to deal with.

While the rest of my delegation busied themselves with unpacking their notes, I abandoned mine and hurried out of the conference room. There wasn't anything on that paperwork worth wasting time on. Vassily hurried to keep up, his long stride eating the distance. I tried to reassure him, or maybe myself, as we walked.

"Could be worse. A stampede of animals is bad, an attack by Prytheen or Zrin raiders would be awful."

"Of course, boss," Vassily said. A little too quick to agree with me, like always. That bland smile hid his thoughts well. But he was a superb administrator, even if he was a yes-man to the core. "Infrared started tracking the stampede ten minutes ago, and now they're close enough to feel."

As though to emphasize his point, the floor shook again. "Why didn't you tell me sooner? Are the inner defenses ready? Where's Torran?"

"Didn't want to interrupt your chance to chew out the captain," Vassily answered. That was as polite about Captain Joyce as I'd ever heard him — once, early on in our working arrangements, he'd called her a word that started with *b* and ended with me promising to fire him the next time he used it. "The militia's reinforcing the inner ultrasound and getting ready to deal with any that punch through. Torran's taken the reaction squad south to check out suspicious signals. Zrin raiders testing the fence, maybe."

Pressing my lips tight together, I managed to hold in the curse that tried to escape my lips. Torran might be a Prytheen warrior, but he'd been loyal to us so far, and he was the best hunter and fighter we had. So of course this disaster struck when he wasn't here to help.

Or he's saving us from a double disaster. A stampede and raiders at the same time? No thanks.

"We'll just have to make do with what we've got," I muttered as I grabbed my laser rifle and checked the charge. So many things I'd had to learn since the Crash — back on Earth, I'd never used a firearm.

Life on Crashland was a quick course on marksmanship.

Outside, Vale Settlement's Main Street stretched out to the left and right. A grand name for a small start, but I had no faith that the *Wandering Star* would ever take us off this rock and someone had to plan for the long term. Along the packed-dirt track stood the few shops the Vale could support. Looking at Akinam's butcher shop, I wondered how much of a bigfur he'd be able to make use of, and how quickly.

If we had to kill any of those giants, I'd rather not let the meat go to waste. And in this heat it would spoil quickly.

Don't count your bigfurs before they're shot, I told myself. There was a reason we didn't hunt them, and why we'd done all we could to keep them out of the Vale. I looked around again, the gathering of colony pods looking as fragile as cardboard.

I didn't need to ask where they were coming from. Even without Vassily telling me the northern defenses had failed, the noise was an unmistakable guide. By the time we arrived at the outskirts of the colony, a dozen nervous members of the colony militia were hard at work hammering posts into the ground. One of them followed behind the rest, activating the ultrasonic fence post by post.

"Will they even notice the ultrasound?" one of them shouted in my direction. That was the only way to be heard over the thunderous rumble of approaching animals.

Sergeant Yates, I reminded myself. Keeping track of the growing settlement was a challenge, one that I might not be up to without the help of my holographic companion, Count Catula. But I did my best to remember people myself, so I let what I knew of Furaha Yates come back to me before I answered.

The big woman had military experience she didn't like to talk about, a temper that scared most people, and a fierce loyalty to her troops that kept them motivated. She was a sergeant by choice — I'd have made her captain if she'd let me, but she'd refused an officer's commission point-blank.

"No idea, Sergeant," I shouted back. "That's why we've got the lasers."

Her laugh was almost lost in the sound of the onrushing stampede. She flashed a bright smile before stabbing another post into the ground. "Wish we had more than rifles."

"Oddly the Arcadia Colony Company wasn't keen on sending us to space with artillery." I settled into cover by a colony pod, powered up my laser, and hoped I wouldn't have to use it.

Yates whistled and pointed, her militia squad hurrying to take cover too. As the ground bounced underfoot, I wondered whether we were fooling ourselves. What cover could keep us safe from the sheer mass of the animals heading for us?

The dust finally parted, and the herd of massive, six-limbed beasts rushed into view. Covered in shaggy white fur, I wondered what had brought them out in the baking midday sun. Whatever it was must be terrifying. The bigfurs were the biggest living things I'd ever seen — bigger than an elephant, bigger than some houses — but still managed to move faster than any car I'd ever driven. The ultrasonic fence seemed a flimsy defense against these white-furred monsters.

So did my laser rifle, if I was honest. I swallowed, took a deep breath, and aimed at the nearest white-furred head. Resting my finger on the trigger, I waited, praying and hoping.

Turn, you fucker, I don't want to have to shoot you, I thought at the approaching animal. It was magnificent, beautiful, deadly, and getting too close. I tightened my finger, taking up the slack in trigger. And then it turned aside, screaming defiance at the invisible barrier it had run into.

Breathing a sigh of relief, I watched the rest of the herd follow their leader and turn away, the dust of their passage blocking out the sun. My hands trembled as I lowered the rifle.

That was when the first spear struck. Sergeant Yates' warning shout was choked off, silenced by the stone-tipped weapon slamming into her chest. Another of the militia froze a moment too long, catching a spear in the side. Alive or dead, he was out of the fight.

I refused to make his mistake, snapping off a shot and diving for cover. Not trying to hit anything, though I wouldn't have complained if I did, but 'first shot *fast*, second shot careful' had been my instructor's advice. You don't need to hit someone to spoil their aim.

Whether because of my shot or simple luck, the spear aimed at me went wide. Everything seemed to slow down around me, my adrenaline-fueled alertness letting me track the arc of the spear back to its origin.

A Zrin clung to the side of one of the bigfurs, half-buried in the creature's fur. Skin as white as the fur he held onto, he was almost invisible. And he wasn't alone.

That was all I had time to see before my dive carried me into the narrow alley between two colony pods. I hit the ground hard, tried to turn it into a roll to my feet, and failed. Instead, I landed with enough force to knock the air out of my lungs and laid there gasping. The Count shimmered in the dust-laden air, meowing at me urgently.

"Yes, fine, fuck," I gasped, pulling myself to my feet and kicking my mind into gear. "Send an emergency alert, we're under attack."

That was as much as I got out before doubling over, coughing. It was enough — the black cat meowed again and my wristband pinged with an urgent signal. I didn't bother checking it, saving my energy for stumbling onward, away from the attackers.

White Zrin? They were blue; everyone knew that. Blue with colored patches. Decent camouflage in the strange shadows of Crashland's purple foliage. Terrible against white fur, or the green of our Earth-plants.

I reached the far end of the alley just as I heard a hissed challenge behind me. My body reacted before my mind did, instinct taking over and spinning me to face the Zrin behind me. A crack of laser fire echoed in the narrow space and the alien warrior dropped like a sack of potatoes. It took me a moment to realize I'd been the one to shoot.

Oh. The laser rifle shook in my hands. I'd never fired at someone before, but luck and training paid off. My assailant lay on the floor, and I wish I could say there was a neat hole burned between the Zrin raider's eyes.

Instead, my blast hit the Zrin's lower chest, leaving my target on the ground in agony. Blood spurted everywhere, and I watched, numb, as the alien struggled to cover the injury. Blood leaked between blue fingers and I heard the anger in the muttered words.

Come on, come on, no time for this. I shouted at myself, turning away and running, putting as much distance between me and the attackers as possible.

CHOKING clouds of dust raised by the stampede filled the air, lending the whole settlement a surreal, hellish tone. Around me, I heard panicking colonists, laser fire, screams — but the dust obscured everything. All I could *see* were silhouettes in the cloud.

"Fall back, back to the colony hub," I shouted, trying to be heard above the tumult. The yellow dust filled my throat and I coughed so hard I almost collapsed. Didn't matter. The colonists were in danger, and if I tore my throat to shreds saving even one of them, I'd take the trade gladly.

Of course, even finding the hub was harder than I'd expected. Without time to adjust and check my location, I stumbled blindly from building to building, trying not to get turned around. Others fled around me, heading inward, and behind us I heard the Zrin pursuing, shouting war cries. If they caught up, that would be the end.

Spotting the sign outside Akinam's saved me, that familiar garish self-portrait of our butcher giving me a landmark to navigate by. Turning left, I saw the enormous dome looming out of the dust clouds.

I focused on that enough to run into a man ahead of me. The small crowd pushed and shoved, trying to get through the door all at once, and I cursed under my breath. Catula shot me a disapproving look, an absurd act that reminded me of where I was and what I should be doing.

"No pushing. One orderly line will get us all inside and trying to shove your way in won't speed things up."

To my surprise, it worked. *I guess my years as a teacher weren't completely wasted, then.* Time spent in a classroom wrangling teenagers was remarkably good practice for running a colony. After a moment, the crowd started moving again, this time steadily. We might get everyone inside before the Zrin caught up.

Or we might not, so I turned to watch for attackers creeping through the clouds of dust. For all that I'd urged the others to keep calm, I couldn't follow my own advice. Heart pounding, hands trembling, I scanned back and forth, watching for any sign of the Zrin.

There. Movement! I didn't waste time thinking. I squeezed the trigger and sent a lance of hot light into the figure emerging from the dust clouds. A hissing snarl told me I'd found my mark — and none too soon, either. Momentum carried the Zrin warrior forward and down at my feet with a hole burnt straight through his throat. Luck rather than skill, but I wouldn't complain about the results. The alien warrior was huge, and I didn't think he needed the spear he carried.

My rifle beeped to let me know it had recharged, and I took the hint to look for other targets as I backed away. Something moved in the dust and I snapped off a shot. No scream, no thud of a body hitting the ground. Either I'd missed, or I'd shot at a figment of my own imagination.

Count Catula hissed, staring in another direction, his fur standing on end. I whirled, couldn't see anything, but fired in the direction he was looking as soon as the rifle beeped again. Perhaps I'd be able to keep the attackers at bay long enough. Maybe. All I could do was try. Others in the crowd joined me, though only four of us were armed and I was uncomfortably aware that if the enemy massed for a charge, we'd be lucky to kill a few of them before they reached us.

The retreat seemed to go on forever, though checking Count Catula's logs later showed it took less than a minute. Back away, hear the beep, take a shot at whatever might be an alien attacker. Repeat, over and over, until I was in the doorway. Rain began falling around me, enormous drops hitting the ground hard and starting to clear the air.

Out of the dust, Zrin appeared. Dozens of them, far too many to shoot, and several armed with bows or javelins. The laser outranged them comfortably, which would have been a much bigger comfort if they weren't already so close. No wonder they'd waited — rushing us would have gotten some of them killed. Now they had the undeniable upper hand.

A hand grabbed my belt and yanked, pulling me back into the building as the heavy metal door slid shut. Not a moment too soon, either — arrows that would have impaled me clattered off the door instead.

3

TZARON

$\mathcal{M}$y warband and I dropped from the side of our drogara mounts, feeling the same unnatural dread that sent them running around the invaders' settlement rather than through it. But where the drogara are mere animals, we Zrin have reason and will — we can resist our instincts.

Easy to say, but each step toward the settlement felt like a step into my own doom. A terrible sound at the edge of my hearing grated on my very soul, promising destruction. Surely whatever sorcerers laid this curse had more and worse magic waiting for those who breached it? I led my followers to a fate worse than death if we continued on this path.

With a shudder, I suppressed those thoughts and pushed on into the curse-laden settlement. The human magic did its work well, Zrin after Zrin falling back, clutching protective amulets and offering prayers to the Sky Gods. By the time I came to the metal stakes that marked the boundary of the human settlement I walked alone, every fiber of my being telling me to flee. I pretended not to notice it, striding through the fence as though it had no effect on me.

That was easier once my back was to my followers. I no longer needed to maintain a tight control on my ssav, keeping the white of fear from showing on my scales.

"Victory," I called at the top of my voice. "We have breached their dwelling place, defeated their guards. All that remains is to take the loot we have earned."

And survive whatever curses are placed on it. That wouldn't be a morale boost, so I left it unsaid and strode on, careless of any enemies who might wait inside. *I* wouldn't shame my warriors for being held back by the curse, but no warrior wanted to think himself a coward. Watching me ignore the curse would motivate them to prove themselves as brave as I was.

Human defenders lay where they'd fallen, some unconscious, others moaning and grabbing at wounds. They'd slain some Zrin before they fell, and it was a relief to see that the scouts' discipline had held sufficiently to leave them alive. Not enough to keep them here, securing the breach and letting my forces gather. Battle cries and the sounds of demon weapons split the air, along with a background of screams and shouting that I couldn't understand.

What in the Skyless Depths is Heshra doing? She can't win this fight alone. I should have led the charge, been at the front where I could control her scouts. I snarled at myself, pushing such thoughts away. The scouts had to go first. I lacked the secret to controlling my ssav as they did and had no way to blend in with a drogara's fur. Now that I was in the settlement, though, I would take my place in the vanguard. My followers had to see me risking myself in combat, or why would they follow me into war?

A pair of corpses was all that remained of Heshra's force. My tail flicked to and fro as I considered the possibilities. Had Heshra lost control of her troops? Or did she think she could hog the glory by defeating the humans alone? Neither felt right. Heshra had the experience to keep her troops together, and the wisdom not to take on the entire battle with only her scouts. Something had gone badly wrong.

It took a moment to realize that the angry growl I heard came from my own throat. Trying to clear my head and push that emotion aside until I found a use for it, I muttered to myself. "Whatever happened, at least they're winning."

Holding onto that thought, I called for my troops to follow me into the settlement. With my example to follow, their discipline held and they crossed the cursed barrier. We advanced swiftly into the dust-filled air, brushing aside what little resistance we met — most of the humans fled our advance. A few fired their weapons at us as we pushed through, then either ducked into their shelters or were struck down in turn.

"Prisoners, not corpses," I snarled at my troops. "I want them alive."

"They shoot at us," a youth called back, outraged. "Why shouldn't we retaliate?"

Sky Gods save me from the young. All that passion with no experience to temper it. "Because we're invading their home. Because we need prisoners. And most of all, because I command it."

I didn't shout the last, but the warrior flinched as though I'd roared it in his face. It was... Jeshar? My warband had grown to a size where I couldn't remember everyone's name, and I decided not to risk a guess. Clapping him on the shoulder, I pointed him inward.

"We are here for greater treasure than the glory of killing these weak soft-skins," I told him. "They have knowledge worth a thousand times the risks we take, and treasure besides. Even the Temple Tribe doesn't have the magics the humans carelessly abandon."

My gaze met his, and I made him my only focus for a moment. His quick nod was enough to show newfound conviction on his part, and a glance at the other warriors in earshot told me they'd listened well too.

Once, that would have been everyone who mattered. Now, it was but a fraction of my band. I'd just have to hope that the others' discipline held.

The sound of humans' weapons intensified ahead, and Zrin cries of pain with them. The air thick with dust, I couldn't see the humans as more than shadowy silhouettes, not enough to attack accurately. But their weapons stabbed out again and again, and while most missed their targets, it was enough to keep my Zrin from closing the gap. The shouts of other warbands sounded flat through the thick air, Gessar and Krosak and the rest trying to keep order in the chaos of the dust storm we'd unleashed.

"Archers," I called. I wanted as many captives as possible, but we had to stop the shooters. The humans would catch their balance if we gave them a chance, and worse, their reinforcements might appear.

A light beam burned through the air beside my head, leaving a swirling trail of yellow dust. A dangerously clever human taking aim at the sound of my commands, but that cut both ways. My archers returned fire, arrows slicing through the air towards the source of the light in a barrage which didn't have to be accurate. Put enough arrows into the air and some of them will hit.

No scream followed, no curse, not even the sound of someone ducking out of the way. Only the clatter of metal on metal followed by silence. Cautiously stalking forward, we came to the massive central palace of the human settlement, its doors firmly shut.

Fat raindrops struck me as I stared at it and cursed. Our deadline was approaching fast and forcing the metal doors would take too long even if the humans inside offered no other resistance.

If I'd thrown away the drogara for no gain, I'd

have a lot of angry followers tonight. But I wasn't out of moves yet. I hammered my fist on the door and shouted in the Sky Tongue, the holy language the Gods left us. Rumor said that the humans spoke it too, lending credence to the claims that they came from the Sky itself.

"Open the door and leave unarmed. I promise you safety." I showed my teeth, though I had no way to know if the humans would see. My promise was sincere — part of my success as a warlord came from keeping my word. People who'd fight to the death against other foes would parlay with me, knowing I'd keep my promises if they laid down their arms.

Of course, that reputation hadn't spread to the humans yet, but it wasn't as though they had any better choices left.

Silence dragged on, the rain intensified, and my frustration mounted. "My patience grows short. Come out, or we shall destroy the building with all of you in it."

"Fine by me."

I blinked, too stunned to speak for a moment. Not by the voice from nowhere — I'd come here to plunder a magician's lair. I'd have been disappointed if there were no strange spells to guard it. But in all my years as a raider and a warlord, no one had so casually mocked my threats. That the voice was warm, musical, and undeniably female didn't help my composure.

Perhaps the speaker didn't understand? She spoke the Sky Tongue with a strong, if pleasant, accent, and I had no way of telling how well she followed my speech. I tried again, using different words in the hope that it would get through. "You will all die. No one will live. Your souls will go to the afterlife. Wild animals will eat what is left of you. Give up."

"I heard you the first time," the speaker replied and chuckled, but there was an undercurrent of tension beneath the amusement. She hid her fear well, just not well enough. And there was something else about that voice, a tone which sent a shiver down my spine and set my tail swishing side to side. Or would have done, if I hadn't caught myself.

"You don't want to die," I said, trying to reason with this infuriating human. "And you do not have to. Let us in and you'll live."

"Today I'll live," she countered. "Your pillaging will destroy our ability to survive here, and there's no way we'll make the march to another settlement that can support us. If we're going to die anyway, might as well dick you over on our way out."

No Zrin would phrase it that way, but I took her meaning. My hands tightened, claws sliding out, and behind me warriors muttered darkly. My own soldiers, the ones who'd fought beside me for years, were disciplined enough to stay still. The more recent recruits were a different story.

"If you live, you have hope," I said. "Perhaps you will make it to your other settlements, but if I must force my way inside, none of you will survive."

A long pause followed, long enough that I wondered if she'd walked away. I kept still as I could manage, my shoulders tensing. *Five more breaths,* I told myself. *Then we force our way in.*

Before my count reached two, the human female's voice returned. "If you're okay with destroying us, why didn't you do it when I said no the first time? You want something in here, and you want it intact. Let's bargain and see if we can't find a compromise."

My jaw snapped shut and my tail lashed from side to side. *Bargain with a defeated foe, one whose life I hold in my hands? Is she trying to provoke me?*

Worst of all, she had a point. Time wasn't on my side, and I had no way to know if my plan to force our way in would work. She had a stronger bargaining position than most, though that didn't mean it was good. "So far, I have taken prisoners rather than slain your kind wherever possible. Surrender, or I will have my men kill those of you that fell into my hands."

Her shrug was almost audible. "They're dead anyway, and I have no reason to trust you to spare them. So, let's talk — what do you want? Maybe we can come to a compromise where we both get what we want."

An admirable attempt at sincerity, though a tremor in her voice gave away the fact that she wasn't nearly as sanguine about the lives of her fellow humans as she pretended. Just as I was less willing to murder helpless prisoners than I claimed to be.

With reluctance, I had to admit that I respected the human's tenacity. Despite the awful position I'd put her in, she refused to give up. She'd fight to the last with all the tools at her disposal, even if they were only words, staking not just her life but the lives of her companions as well. And I could listen to that warm, soft voice until the Sky Gods returned.

"Very well, let us speak," I said, making my mind up. It could not hurt to keep talking while my followers prepared more forceful matters. "I am here for your magic, your wisdom."

Another pause, this one brief. "You mean our

technology? We can do that, but I don't know if you will understand it — little of it is in the Sky Tongue. I'll give you all we have, though."

Outraged sounds behind her, chatter in a human language. Not a word made sense to me, though the gist was clear: her companions were unhappy with the bargain, and they were arguing. My lips pulled back in a snarl and I punched the metal wall of the building hard enough to ring it like a bell.

"Enough bickering," I said. "You offered a bargain and I will take it, with one change."

The argument cut off, the humans settling into a nervous hush.

"Your magic is worthless to me if I can't understand it. I want an interpreter with it. I want *you.*"

4

VICTORIA

*T*oo shocked to answer, I stared at the speaker. Time stretched as I tried to come up with a response that wasn't just babble.

Vassily broke the silence in the control room. "You have to take the deal, Victoria, you have to."

His smug superiority had vanished, and rather than the confident if arrogant young man he'd been, I saw a man on the edge of full-blown panic. Eyes bulging, sweat pouring down his face, a face that was white as a sheet. In one hand he held a handker-chief, damp with the sweat he'd mopped from his forehead. In the other... I struggled not to laugh. Out of all the tools on hand, he'd chosen a fruit knife? How useful did he think that would be?

"Preposterous," Mr. Powry broke in, his English

accent lending him an air of authority. He, at least, had a laser rifle in hand. I allowed myself a brief hope — perhaps this meant the more level-headed members of the colony were on my side?

Powry dashed that hope before it had fully formed. "We can't turn over our technology to the Zrin. They are enough of a danger to the colony already. No, unacceptable. Ms. Bern, you will simply have to negotiate something else. Perhaps our cultural data instead."

His total self-assurance, along with that accent, made his demand seem almost reasonable. Almost. "You think these brutes are going to trade our safety for a Shakespeare collection? And how do you think that brute is going to threaten you with the schematics for a laser rifle, Mr. Powry? Bludgeon you to death with them? Because I can say with confidence that he won't be making lasers."

Snapping at him was satisfying, if perhaps unwise. Powry's lean face turned bright red as I stared him down, and he spluttered his reply. "We cannot take chances with the colony's safety. If no deal is possible, we shall simply have to wait for Torran and his men to come to the rescue."

"Abandoning the Zrin's captives to die." I kept my breathing steady with an effort that, in a just world, would have earned me a medal. "Colonists we're responsible for."

Powry shrugged. "They may already be dead, and we must be mindful of the colonists who are safe in here with us. Open the doors and the Zrin might storm in to kill us all."

"No, no, she's right," Vassily weaseled into the conversation. "We have to take the deal, it's our only chance to — for the colony to survive."

I'd have appreciated his support if it hadn't been so obviously self-serving. Vassily wasted no time looking for another answer to the problem, his fingers flying over a keyboard, dumping files into a pocket datastore without even looking at what he was including. Powry turned on him, lips thin and pale, voice hot and angry.

"Keep out of this, boy," he snapped. "The adults are talking and it's none of your business."

Vassily's eyes narrowed and he turned to face Powry, lifting his fruit knife again. Anger replaced the fear in his eyes as he took a knife-fighter's stance, his blade pointing at Powry's throat. That little blade didn't look quite so comical anymore. Powry took a step back and adjusted his grip on his rifle, not quite pointing it at Vassily, but getting too close for comfort.

"That's enough, both of you," I said, loud and firm, stepping between them. "Your bickering isn't helping, and we've got others to look out for. It's my ass on the line, so let me think."

"Now, Ms. Bern, we have to consider this logically," Powry said at the same moment Vassily tried, "Look, no, you have to go. It's the only way to make sure the rest of the colonists are safe."

His eyes darted to the door and his tongue emerged to lick his lips. I understood his nerves: the last time this many colonists had gathered in one building was the Big Meeting, just after the Crash, and that came close to turning violent. This time, surrounded by hostile aliens, would be worse.

There was space for everyone — this was one of the three colony mega-pods, each intended to form the core of a city. The stasis chamber had held me and more than a thousand others on the ill-fated mission to Arcadia, and there was living space for more. It wouldn't be comfortable, but that wouldn't be the problem.

Vassily, to his credit, had called Torran as soon as he realized what was happening. But with the storm blowing in we couldn't count on the flier bringing him and the militia back today, and until they arrived, morale was fragile. We had plenty of food, if you could call the sludge that came out of the makers food, but water? Maybe, with luck, a couple of days' worth, and everyone knew it. Plus there were colonists caught outside, either prisoners of the Zrin or on the run without supplies. Anyone with family stuck out there would want this over and their loved ones safe. If they had to throw me to the Zrin to make that happen... well, some of them would regret doing it. Others would jump at the chance. I couldn't even blame them — unlike the two assholes sharing the control room with me, who were trying to save themselves.

Focus, Victoria. Options. One: stay here, everyone dies. We'll call that a failure. Anything else had to be better.

Two: Torran returns with his troops and there's a fight which ends with deaths on both sides and the settlement on fire. Also a failure.

Three: ask the colonists to vote on the deal. Start a mini-riot which probably ends with me being thrown outside. No thanks.

Four: ... *God dammit.*

I didn't see any other choice.

"Give me that," I said, grabbing the portable from Vassily and turning to the door. Powry stepped into my path, a pinched scowl on his narrow face.

"I'm sorry, Victoria, but I can't allow you to do this." He seemed genuinely sad, which was a bit of a surprise. "That data, in the wrong hands, could be the death of us all."

"Mr. Powry, can you think of another way out of this, one that doesn't involve everyone dying? I can't, and believe me I've tried."

Maybe the alien barbarians would be a relief after these two. Exasperation served me better than fear, and I shoved him aside. Physical contact shocked Powry out of my way, as though he couldn't believe that I'd disobey him. That anyone, especially a girl, would ignore him and his threats hadn't crossed Mr. Powry's mind.

"Wait," he called after me, the pitch of his voice rising. Ignoring him, I pushed on through the crowded corridor. The closer I got to the door, the fewer people stood in my way — no one wanted to be close to the door if the aliens forced their way inside. Those behind me muttered amongst themselves, their eyes on my back. If I gave them time to think about what I was doing, they'd grab me to stop me letting the aliens in.

So I didn't give them a chance. Swiping my wristband over the door control, I overrode the emergency locks and stepped out into the dust-covered street, my hands spread wide to show I was unarmed. Behind me, the door snapped shut, and I tried to ignore the sudden feeling of doom filling me as I looked at my captors.

No enemies tried to rush the door while it was open, which meant there was a chance their leader would keep his word. It was the only good news. Dozens of Zrin watched me step forward, and I hadn't realized how big they were. The shortest of them was tall by human standards, and most of them were seven foot tall or more. And all of that height was muscle covered in blue skin, or rather scales, marked with the strange moving patterns they called ssavs. I'd read the reports about them and how they showed the Zrins' emotions, though I hadn't paid enough attention to what the colors meant. I hoped amber and green meant something good, because those were the only colors that greeted me.

Amongst them stood their captives. I looked at them, surprised to see Sergeant Yates supporting another militiaman. Wounded but alive, the two of them struggled to stay upright. Despite their condition, I felt a rush of relief at the sight — I'd assumed they'd died in the opening attack. A second reason to hope the alien leader would keep his word. Yates scowled, eyes narrow, unimpressed by her captors. She shot me a look that was all too easy to read. 'You can't trust them,' it said. 'Don't give them what they want.'

Tough. I was the one who decided what bargains to strike, and if this was the cost of saving her and the rest of the colonists, then so be it.

The die was cast — it was too late to go back now. Taking a deep breath, I walked toward the band of raiders.

One Zrin stepped forward to meet me, tall even by their standards and broad-shouldered too. He drew in all my attention the way a candle flame draws a moth. Muscles rippled under scaled skin as he moved, powerful yet graceful, and I caught myself biting my lower lip as I looked at his six pack. With an effort, I resisted the temptation to run my hands over it, to feel the muscles at play.

Without conscious decision, my gaze crept lower. He wore a leather kilt with a colorful belt from which a knife hung. Or maybe it was a sword — what looked like a long knife on the alien warrior would be a short sword in my hands.

A bulge swelled beneath the kilt, and I tried not to think about it. A terrible urge rose in me, a desire to see, to touch. I pulled my gaze up, blushing bright red and hoping that the aliens were as bad at reading human body language as I was at reading theirs.

His broad, muscular chest made me want to press myself against it, and his hands... strong, dexterous fingers flexed, and it was impossible to stop myself imagining what they'd feel like on my skin, under my clothes, holding me down.

At last my gaze reached his rugged face, inhuman but even more attractive for that. Like the rest of him, there wasn't an ounce of spare fat to be seen. A lean, hungry face, violet eyes staring at me as though he wanted to eat me up.

My blush deepened at the thought, and I bit my lip hard enough to make myself wince. *Snap out of it, woman, you need to focus.* He might be gorgeous, but that didn't mean he was a good guy. He'd invaded my home, he was a warlord and a killer, he was not appropriate lust material.

Not that it mattered to my body, but I had to ignore that and focus. I was here and at his mercy. Time to see if he had any.

"I surrender."

5

TZARON

*B*lood of the Sky Gods, she was beautiful. I'd loved her voice from the moment I heard its warmth, but the beauty of her face and body eclipsed even that. I stood, stunned, my eyes locked on hers. A deep blue, like distant pools of water, or gemstones of unsurpassed quality. They were like no eyes I'd ever seen, though I recognized the fiery intensity in her gaze. She watched me with an intense interest equal to my own, and I felt my blood heat. The urge to forget everything else, to snatch her up and carry her away, or even to take her here in front of everyone, almost overwhelmed me.

Her words broke through my paralysis, more for the sound of her voice than its content. As much as I'd liked the sound alone, seeing her speak and hearing her words together was better than either alone had prepared me for. I closed my mouth with a snap and tried to focus on answering her.

It wasn't easy. Her body, small and frail-looking, didn't match her confident walk. Hair the color of flames, long and unbound, flowed down over her shoulders like a river of fire. Her lips, a bright red, drew me in. She wore far too much clothing for my liking — it hid her shape, making me want to tear it off. But perhaps that was a cunning human trick? I saw enough of her curves to hint at the shapes under the fabric, distracting me.

If that was her plan, it worked too well. She spoke again, repeating her surrender with an air of exasperation, and that was what finally snapped me back to reality.

"I accept," I said, as gravely as I could. "You are my guest now."

"Prisoner," she corrected, lips curling as she pushed the word out at me. "I'm no guest, I'm a prisoner."

My jaw tightened at her blunt refusal of my courtesy and offer of protection, but there was no time to discuss it. "Prisoner or guest, call it what you will. Come with me now."

She didn't move. "Where are you taking me?"

Rain fell in earnest now, dark clouds racing across the sky promising worse to come. No time for debate, especially not with the rest of her guards on the way. Ignoring her question, I stepped closer and threw her over my shoulder, turning to my troops and snarling at them.

We all knew the plan, and it did not include standing here staring at our captive. Besides which, I didn't want any of them looking at her. That was a feeling I'd have to think about later, when I had time to spare. Right now, we had to leave.

As soon as I gave the signal, my warriors turned and ran back the way we'd come, leaving the human prisoners but keeping what loot they'd gathered. Wind howled around us, and that wasn't all that howled. My captive made a surprising amount of noise as she battered my back with her small fists. Hard enough to feel, not enough to slow me down.

Reaching the settlement's edge we faced the demon fence once again and fear bit deep into us. All around me, Zrin struggled with an urge to panic, some with more grace than others. A few staggered to a halt, shouting warnings to the rest of us, trying to save us from the 'curse'. Holding my human captive over my shoulder, I freed my right arm to grab those who froze in fear and shove them forward. I wasn't about to leave anyone behind, not even if I had to throw them across the boundary.

A second time I led by example, confronting the boundary myself and forcing myself across. Once on the far side, the unnatural dread receded, elation rising to replace it. Who else could say they'd raided the humans and escaped? No other warlord under the Sky had that claim to fame.

Glancing back to check that all my troops followed, I saw a dark spot in the distant sky. The humans' flying machine, racing back to save its base and hunt us down. As I watched, a gust of wind sent it tumbling sideways. As I'd planned, the wind would slow our pursuers and the rain would blind them.

"Too late, demons," I cried, my voice swallowed by the rising wind. "Try keeping up with us in the storm, come on. The thunder spirits will break your metal bird like an egg."

Rain fell almost horizontally, the wind whipping it into a painful assault like a thousand tiny sling stones. I shifted the human to my other shoulder, shielding her from the rain's assault and wondering how humans faced the world each day when the weather itself would slice straight through their soft hides. Was that why they wore so much clothing?

I caught up with the trailing elements of the warband, a pair of scouts carrying a body between them. It took a moment to recognize Heshra without her usual poise and attitude, but that was her. Blood mixed with the rain, flowing from a wound in her chest, and I swore under my breath.

"What happened?" I shouted over the wind. It took two goes to get their attention, then one of the youths turned his head and answered.

"Don't know. We broke through the curse-wall, the humans fought back and it was chaos."

"Couldn't see her. Went looking." His companion was terse but enlightening. "Found her like this."

I bit back the curses that came to my mind. She was far from perfect, but she was also the lynchpin that kept the scouts loyal to my warband. Without her, would they even stay together? "Is she—"

"Dead?" Heshra croaked the question, barely audible. "Tough luck. You'll not get rid of me this easily, Tzaron."

Caught between relief and annoyance, I forced a laugh. "Heshra, I'd never wish you dead. I need your scouts, and we couldn't have done this without you."

"Just you remember that when you're spreading the loot around," she said, voice strained and quiet, hard to hear over the sound of the storm. Exhausted from the effort of speaking, Heshra let her head droop, wet hair falling to hide her face. I prayed she'd make it to safety.

And that I'd played the odds right — otherwise there'd be no safety for either of us to reach. No point in worrying about that, though, not now that I'd set my course. Either my plan worked, or it didn't. We lived or we died.

Lightning cracked above us, the thunder's boom hitting at the same moment. The downpour was heavy now, a pounding ice-cold force that made me wince as it bit into my skin. My human captive struggled to cover her face, wrapping her arms around her head and shouting something incoherent.

Ahead of us, trees loomed out of the veil of rain like dark sentinels offering safety. Putting my head down, I ran in amongst the branches that whipped back and forth in the storm. An exultant joy built in my chest as I carried my prize deeper amongst the trees, out of sight of the sky and the vengeful eyes of those aboard the metal flying beast.

DEEP IN THE FOREST, the trees overhead sheltered us from the storm and we slowed to a comfortable run, one that we could keep up for hours or even days. According to the priests the storm would take days to pass, and I intended to make good use of that time.

The camp, when we reached it, was already filled with happy warriors waving around their loot. A few held up human weapons, more had metal parts that might be forged into fine blades or strong armor. Others had taken trade goods, luxuries like human clothing. None of it would fit a Zrin, except perhaps a child, but somebody would find a use for the wonderful materials it was made of. Rich treasures indeed, but thing compared to the human I carried.

And the wisdom she carries, I reminded myself. This raid hadn't just been to get me a female, it was to strengthen my whole warband with human magic. Getting her was a spur-of-the-moment addition to the plan, not the goal.

Stopping just short of the camp proper, I lifted her from my shoulder, planting her feet on the ground and ignoring her glare. "We are safe now. There is a little time to talk."

She put her hands on her hips, bared her teeth, and looked up at me as though she might at any moment bite out my throat. Tiny, weak, soaked through by the rain, she still managed to be intimidating. *She practiced that,* I realized, impressed by her skill.

"Safe?" The word shot from her mouth like an arrow, pushed out by pure rage. "You think you're safe? Torran will track you down and kill you for this. If you send me back right now—"

"—You'll get lost in the storm and die," I interrupted, claws extending and tail swinging too fast. Keeping my emotions under control was second nature to me, but this human didn't make it easy. "And your Torran will have no trail to follow by the time the storm passes. I have no time to waste on this. Who are you?"

"I am Victoria Bern, *Colony Coordinator* for the *Arcadia Colony Company,* and duly elected *Speaker of the Vale Settlement* you just raided. And who the hell are you?"

Most of those words meant nothing to me, titles or names not in Sky Tongue. Her own language was sweet as honey, and even those few words made me want to hear more of it.

"I am Tzaron, High Lord of this Warband, Ruler of the Skyfallen by right of conquest, peerless warrior and fearless ruler." Normally I was proud of my titles, all earned. The human — *Victoria* — rolled her eyes, taking a lot of the pleasure from the recitation.

"Nice titles. None of them will protect you."

Infuriating creature. My blood boiled with conflicting desires; my shoulders ached from the tension in them. How did she get under my skin so easily?

"I have planned for pursuit," I told her, struggling not to tell her the details of my preparations. She didn't need to know, and I didn't need to impress her with my efforts. As much as I told myself that, the urge was hard to ignore. "I have much work to do after a victory like this, and I cannot keep you with me for it without danger. You surrendered to me — can I trust you to stay put? I do not wish to bind you or keep another Zrin out here with you. You have no hope of you finding your way back to your settlement alone, so it would be stupid to run off."

She screwed up her face but nodded. Good. "Do not come into the space beyond these trees. If you have need of me, call out and I will hear."

Another reluctant nod. That would have to do. Victoria slumped against the nearest tree, hugging herself and shivering, and reminding me that humans fared far worse in the cold than Zrin did. That, at least, I could do something about — digging into my pack, I found a blanket and passed it to her along with a strip of jerky.

"Warm yourself. I will return when the rituals are complete."

It was harder than it should have been to turn my back on her and walk into the waiting crowd, but there were formalities to observe and rituals to be upheld. Things that meant the world to my people, so they mattered to me.

Warriors cheered me as I walked among them, and I congratulated each on their loot and their success. Some who'd lost friends in the raid were angry or despondent instead of triumphant, and I stopped to commiserate with them. But casualties had been light, few had lost loved ones, and the general mood was one of celebration.

"Friends," I cried out as I leaped onto the stump of a fallen tree. "We have a victory over the human Sky Demons. We have conquered! Not even their wisdom can stand against us."

"Against *you*," Krosak called from in amongst the throng. He might be shortsighted, but he knew his role in this ritual well. "You led us to victory, Lord Tzaron."

Others took up the cry, and soon the entire encampment shook to the sound of my name, shouted over and over. I held up my hands, face turned aside as though embarrassed by the praise, and they quieted slowly.

"No, my friends," I demurred. "Victory belongs to us all, so let us share the spoils of war."

One by one, the warriors approached me, placing their spoils in a neat pile before me. I greeted each warrior by name, announced their tribute for everyone to hear, finding something to laud in each offering. Sometimes that was tricky, but not today. The spoils were rich — I'd seen bigger piles, but this one was almost entirely prizes of great value.

It took till nightfall for that part of the victory rite to end, not that it was clear with the heavy storm clouds above the forest's thick canopy. Water dripped through, but at least we were sheltered from the worst of the downpour.

But those who'd stayed back to keep the camp had done their jobs well. A pile of firewood, stacked under the thickest cover available, would warm us and keep us from being too miserable as the night wore on.

And wear on it did. The trouble with a small pile of valuables is that it's hard to divide fairly, and the work of a warband leader often comes down to sharing the loot out well — while keeping back as much as possible to trade. A delicate balance, and a difficult one, but I had experience navigating this problem. Everything went well — until a voice rang out from the back of the crowd.

"What about the human female you took?" Gessar. Not someone I could afford to ignore; he was a warrior of great renown and the leader of the largest sub-band of my horde. A pity he was also a tradition-minded fool. "Why isn't she on the loot-pile, eh? You hold out on your followers, Lord Tzaron?"

"She is not loot. She is an interpreter of the wisdom we have taken and will benefit us all." I stopped short of saying 'that was the whole point of this raid, idiot' but it wasn't easy. "She is mine, for the good of all."

Others took up Gessar's cry. Older raiders mostly, those who hewed to the old traditions. No one who would actually care who ended up with the female, but plenty who wanted me cut down to size or enforce old rules for the sake of it. I refused to bow to such pressure.

And yet, I had to say *something*. My own supporters shouted back, tempers flared on both sides, and if I didn't intervene quickly, blood would be shed. Untangling the network of feuds that followed a brawl would take too long and cost too many lives.

I growled, the sound cutting through the rising argument and silencing most of the crowd. The remainder lowered their voices, eyeing me nervously as I stepped forward into the firelight.

"I am no thief, to steal from my own followers after a successful raid," I said, meeting Gessar's gaze and staring him down. "You may dislike my methods, but you are here because I lead you to success and profit, yes? New ideas, change, these things can be frightening. If you no longer wish to follow me, take your share and go in peace. If not, then *shut up and listen to me.*"

The last words came out as a roar, shocking Gessar into taking a step back. He stood half a head taller than me and broader in the shoulders, a tall block of muscle covered in battle scars. Looking like that, he wasn't used to anyone standing up to him. Not even the warlord he'd pledged his forces to.

"I never said that you were a thief," he protested. "Just that if we're to share the spoils equally, we should all get—"

I cut him off, taking a step closer. Inside each

other's reach now, either of us could strike the other down too quickly to be stopped.

"She is not loot," I repeated, voice a low, menacing hiss. "I have told you twice now. The third time, I will carve it into your heart because your brain obviously can't take in the lesson."

Another step forward, and he took one back, his ssav a writhing mass of confused colors. White and red, amber and gray, the lines crossed and merged and split in a dizzying display.

I was making an enemy here, a dangerous one. But I hadn't clawed my way to my position to take an over-muscled idiot's 'advice' on how I should do things. If I let him get the idea he could dictate to me, Gessar wouldn't stop there. A Zrin with his ambition never would.

More importantly, the notion of treating my prisoner as no more than a prize to be passed off or claimed made my blood burn like molten rock. No one would look at her that way — not without feeling my claws in their throat.

"Peace, lord, peace," Gessar said, sounding as startled as I was by the passion his objections raised in me. "If you need her for your plans, then take her. For the good of the horde."

A muffled chuckle spread through the crowd. I

forced myself to ignore it, clapping Gessar on the shoulder. He'd backed down. That was what mattered, and I had no reason to humiliate him by mocking his choice. No need to start a feud with his kin and followers. The amusement of some of the crowd was odd, but better to leave it be for now and let any frustration fade before working out what was so funny.

Turning my back on Gessar, I walked back to the fire. All around, my people went back to their celebrations, and I thought the drama of the evening was over. Now was the time for telling tall tales of the battle, of telling those who'd kept the camp ready about the battle they'd missed out on. Some slipped away in pairs (or in one case, an adventurous trio) to celebrate more privately. Krosak thrust a skin of strong berrywine into my hand, and I felt some of the tension leave my shoulders. The raid was a success, and I could finally afford to relax.

The Sky Gods loved to mock overconfidence. As I drank my first mouthful, a warrior burst back into the meeting, hurriedly adjusting her kilt. "Sire! Your human has run off."

*N*o sooner was Tzaron out of sight than my thoughts turned to escape. He'd made valid points about how dangerous leaving on my own was, but his argument neglected one important fact. I didn't care about the danger, not when the alternative was being dragged off to god knew what fate. Better to die trying to get home.

"Count Catula, where are we?" The hologram shivered into existence, blue light leaking around the edges of his sleek black form. Eerier than ever in these dark woods, he looked up at me with glowing blue eyes and meowed.

Between us, a map appeared, showing the Vale Settlement in fine detail. Zooming out, a trail appeared — Catula's tracing of our route. What started as a solid line soon branched out into a fuzzy fan of possibilities. Companion AIs had navigation skills, but they were programmed for Arcadia, not Crashland, and Arcadia had satellites overhead for GPS. Here, as soon as we left the area around the settlement, he relied on dead reckoning and luck to guide me.

Could be worse, I told myself. *At least he's willing to admit he doesn't know where we are. That's better than 95% of male navigators I've had to put up with.*

By Catula's best guess, the shortest route back toward the Vale would be off to my left. Not the direction we'd come from, nowhere near. I looked into the dark shadows between the trees, dubious. "I guess it makes sense. They were trying to hide the trail to their camp."

Catula tilted his head to the side, offering no opinion, and I realized I was stalling. I had a choice to make — follow my memory, follow his directions, or to stay put and hope for the best.

I crossed out number three without a thought. *The first duty of a prisoner is to escape,* I recited to myself, though where I'd read that I didn't know. Hopefully, in the memoirs of someone who'd escaped. This would be the best chance I'd get: every day spent traveling with the Zrin would take me further from home. With the Zrin distracted by their victory feast, I'd never have a better opportunity.

Something deep argued, but I didn't listen. Sure, my captor was hot. Hot enough to burn. The kind of sexy that made my legs weak and my body tingle. But that didn't make him a good guy, or on my side. I had enough experience with men to know that the hot ones could be assholes too.

Sure, I wanted to feel his arms around me again, but I refused to let that keep me from escaping while I had the opportunity. The next time a loud roar went up from the Zrin party, I used it to cover the sounds of getting to my feet and following Count Catula down the path he'd indicated.

'Path' might be a strong word for it. I hadn't gone far before it vanished into the undergrowth. Not the best start to my escape, perhaps, but I tried to look on the bright side. If I didn't disturb the plants, it might make following my trail tricky. I had to keep an eye out for positives here. There weren't very many of them.

Slow and careful, I inched my way along until the sounds of the party faded behind me, then picked up the pace. My morning exercise run taking me around the Vale Settlement hadn't prepared me for this. Unfamiliar plants tangled my feet as I ran, branches whipped at my face, and I remembered all the reports I'd read about Crashland's wildlife. If I ran into a pack of tree-hunters, or worse, a tenger, my escape would end in a bloody mess.

Sucks, but there's no choice. Not if I ever want to be free again. And it'll make a fine tale for the grandkids.

I snorted at the thought. That would mean having kids first, and *that* needed me to find a man who'd make a good father. So far, no joy there. Maybe it would be a good story with which to entertain someone else's grandkids?

Something pulled at my heart, and I studiously ignored it. Yes, the raider warlord was beautiful, dangerous, and rough in all the right ways. *No,* that didn't make him someone to consider as a potential father of my children. But would my body listen? It would not. It had another agenda, one that involved being pinned by that big blue hunk of muscle and finding out exactly what he had under that kilt.

Distracted by the battle with my own hormones, I didn't notice the change in the ground until my foot sank in and wouldn't come free. I stopped hard, grabbing a tree for balance rather than fall and twist my ankle. Firm earth had given way to soft moss, and even in the darkness under the trees I saw my footprints stretching out behind me. A trail no one could miss, leading straight to me.

I weighed my choices. Retreat, and potentially run headlong into the Zrin who were bound to be chasing me by now? Or press on, not knowing how far this mossy marsh kept going or how deep it got? Either way, I'd leave an easy trail to follow.

"I'm not going back," I said. The storm answered with a boom of thunder that shook the trees. Wood creaked and wind howled, but I grinned, an idea forming.

The moss gripped my boots, slowing me, and I cursed under my breath continuously as I made my way deeper into it. My search took longer than I liked, but eventually I found what I was looking for — a branch hanging low enough to reach, thick enough that I thought it would hold my weight but not a Zrin's.

"What do you think, Count?" I whispered, only to get a confused look from the hologram. Some things were too far from his area of expertise to even guess at, and how much weight an alien tree branch could hold was one of them.

"Guess I'll just have to try it and see," I muttered, reaching up to grip the branch and pull it down. The weird roughness of whatever passed for bark on it dug into my hand, uncomfortable but not painful, and the branch creaked but didn't snap.

With a grunt of effort, I tried my first chin-up since school. Not that I'd really managed them there, either. But fear for my life was a great motivator, and with a heave I pulled myself up, nearly fell, recovered enough to hook a leg over the branch, and held on for dear life.

Stage one of plan complete. On its own, it just made me a fruit to be plucked by the first Zrin to find me. Either that or a piñata, depending how they treated runaways here. I still had to get out of sight. Hanging upside down at a Zrin's eye level wouldn't help unless it paralyzed my captors with laughter.

"Come on, get a fucking move on," I whispered to myself, straining to pull myself along the rough surface. Getting on top of the branch was out of the question, and even this awkward shuffle left me unsure how long I'd keep my grip. I was on the verge of giving up when I heard my pursuers. Blood-chilling yells sent adrenaline pumping through my veins and I redoubled my efforts. Whatever it cost me, I'd pay the bill later.

Still upside down, I dragged myself along the branch, the rough surface gripping my clothes. At least my clothing protected me from the abrasive bark — I felt the leg of my pants tear as I dragged my leg over a patch of spines growing from the tree and shuddered at the thought that it could have been my leg. I hoped no telltale threads stuck to the branch, but it was better than leaving a blood trail.

After an eternity of pulling myself along, I reached the tree trunk and managed to get myself right-side-up on the branch. Blood rushed from my head and a wave of dizziness almost dropped me to the ground, but I grabbed hold of another branch with one hand and clung to it until I recovered my balance. Thunder cracked overhead, and I tried to read that as a good omen.

With an effort, I put the thought that I'd climbed a tree in a thunderstorm out of my mind. For all I knew, this was the tallest tree for miles around. The next flash of lightning might strike it, an embarrassing and fatal end to my escape.

Okay, so I didn't *succeed* in putting that out of my mind. But I tried, pulling myself up to stand in the branches and making my way from one to the next, looking for a sturdy path to another tree, and then another. It was slow going, testing branches before putting weight on them, creeping along from tree to tree, and in other circumstances I'm sure the Zrin would have heard me from miles away. But the storm winds shook the canopy and the thunder boomed, covering any noise I made.

Eventually, the ground beneath the trees looked solid again and, after a cautious poke with a stick to confirm we'd left the moss, I dropped to the ground, collapsed against the nearest tree, and sucked in air.

When I'd slowed from hyperventilating to merely panting for air, I pushed off the tree and started following Catula at something between a fast walk and a jog. I wasn't making good time, especially not when I kept stumbling and clinging to trees for balance, but I was moving away from the hunters, and the sound of their cries soon receded into the distance. My trick worked, I thought, exulting in the fact that I'd given those seasoned Zrin hunters the slip. Now, no one knew where I was.

Including me, but no change there.

Count Catula's faint blue glow illuminated the undergrowth around him as he led me in what I hoped was the right direction. That was the only reason I saw movement, the dark purple leaves twitching. I froze, staring, not sure what to do.

The creature that pounced from the darkness of the stormy night didn't give me time to decide. A blur of dark motion, too fast to make out, it landed with two clawed front paws ripping and tearing.

Lucky for me, the glowing cat held its attention. Catula's image fritzed into static as deadly paws passed through him, then reformed in an instant. The creature looked down almost comically, trying to work out what had gone wrong with its attack.

I took that moment of confusion to duck behind a nearby tree. I doubted it would do much good — as a predator, the attacker probably had good hearing and my heart was pounding loud enough to wake the dead.

It bought me a little time to think, though I didn't know what to spend it on. Running would be pointless. Would Catula scare the monster off? Or was there a way to fight back? I didn't see anything to use as a weapon and fighting bare-handed would be suicide. Maybe fighting a 'ghost' would frighten it away, but that didn't seem likely. Catula was too small and harmless.

What would Sun Tzu have done here? I'd read the master strategist's book years ago, and all I remembered was his advice to not fight in a swamp. Great advice assuming you weren't trapped in one when the wildlife decided you looked like a nice meal.

My thoughts were interrupted by a patch of silence to my right. The forest was full of noises, most of which I'd tuned out until they stopped.

Trembling, clenching my jaw to keep my teeth from chattering, I turned my head to see another one of the creatures padding out of the shadows toward me. At least, I thought it was the same species as the one 'fighting' Catula. I couldn't see either of them well enough to be certain, and this wasn't the time to be classifying the wildlife.

Some people would say I'm too analytical, and times like these I tend to agree with them.

While my brain was locked up being stupid-smart, my body was more practical. Before my thoughts caught up, I'd started backing away, opening the distance between me and the monster. It wouldn't be enough to save me, but it was all I could do.

Away from Catula's light, making out details was impossible. As black as the shadows it walked through, all I could make out clearly were the creature's eyes. Cold, hard yellow eyes watched me and it hissed, a blood-curdling sound. Those hungry eyes were perhaps three feet from the ground and the shadowy form rose higher behind them. I wracked my brain for any advice, anything I'd read about surviving an animal attack. Most of what came to mind was 'don't look like prey' and 'make yourself look big.'

Great advice for someone who isn't scrambling away on her back, I thought as lightning cracked overhead. Even through the trees, it illuminated my hunter — a bulky predator with six limbs, dark coarse fur, and needle-sharp teeth. Something like a big cat crossed with a small bear, it had the cuteness of neither and the deadliness of both.

And worse, there were more behind it. At least two. I'd stumbled into a pack hunter's territory, and now I'd die here.

At least that will leave Zrin a mystery they'll never solve.

My hand landed on a fallen branch and an absurd burst of hope flashed through me. A weapon wouldn't save me, but at least it gave me the strength to fight. I pulled myself to my feet, lifting the branch like a baseball bat. I didn't know how to fight, but I wasn't about to lie there and wait for death.

As though that was a signal, the nearest monster leaped at me, a pounce so swift it gave me no chance to react. My death soared at me and my brain froze, watching it come as though in slow motion. At the height of its arc, something moved in the corner of my eye, a blur on an intercept course with the monster.

The predator's sharp, hooked claws almost at my

face when the blur hit, leaving me with an impression of surprise and fear on the monster's face as it vanished sideways. Time crashed back to normal, I sucked in a breath, and turned to see what had saved me.

A tenger. One of the most dangerous animals on Crashland, at least that we'd encountered. The size of a big tiger, with black and gray markings and tentacles where its lower face should be. Venomous tentacles at that, now wrapped around the animal that had attacked me. The rest of the pack seemed as startled as I was, turning away from me to the attacker in their midst.

Was a tenger dangerous enough to win against a pack of these bear-monsters? *Doesn't matter,* I told myself. *Let them fight, I'm out of here.*

I didn't wait to watch, just turned and ran. Hisses and roars behind me kept me moving faster than I'd thought possible, ignoring the slap of branches against my face. Even with terror giving me an extra boost of adrenaline, I didn't get far.

I heard the animal before I saw it, a low growl straight ahead, beyond the circle of Catula's light. Skidding to a halt, I flinched back as a tenger pounced from the darkness, falling on my ass again.

The creature landed over me, tentacles writhing, and I thought that I'd at least given this my best shot.

"Sorcha, kreiss." The words meant nothing to me, but the tone of command was impossible to miss and the voice familiar. Incredibly, the tenger obeyed, backing off and leaving me unhurt. I stared for a handful of seconds before remembering to shut my mouth and looked past the monster.

"Sorcha will not hurt you," Tzaron said, switching to the butchered Eskel language we had in common. "She is a good zsinz and does as she is told."

Oh. That's all right then, I thought. And fainted.

7
___

TZARON

I caught the human before her head hit the ground, cursing under my breath as I moved. Her chest still rose and fell with her breath, proving she still lived. That was all I knew. Was this some human malady, or had the kzor hurt her? A quick examination showed no sign of injury, though to be absolutely certain I'd need to undress her.

A medical necessity? I shook my head sharply, to the amusement of Sorcha who hissed a laugh.

"She would not understand," I told my zsinz companion as I slung my captive over my shoulder. "And more kzor may be here any minute."

Sorcha hissed again, a laugh with an edge to it. She'd missed out on the fighting so far, after all — and that didn't sit well with her at all. I grinned at her, waving her onward and wondering how much of what I said she really understood.

"Come on, you take the lead. If the kzor try to circle us, you'll be the one to clear a path. My arms will be full."

Sorcha splayed her tentacles wide, an aggressive gesture showing what she thought of that plan. Nevertheless, she bounded on ahead, keeping me and Victoria safe as we withdrew from the kzor's hunting grounds. To her disappointment, the kzor had no intention of picking a fight with a zsinz and didn't bother us on our way out.

Soon Victoria began squirming in my arms, pushing ineffectually at my chest and trying to escape my grip. I let out a breath and whispered a prayer of thanks to the Sky Gods. If she struggled, she couldn't be that badly hurt.

"Still," I commanded. To my surprise, Victoria obeyed. Trembling in my arms, she stopped resisting, letting me carry her back to the camp. Cradling her body against mine, feeling the firm softness of her flesh and the warmth of her body, it was impossible to resist the human's appeal. By the time I returned to camp and set her down in my tent, I was as hard as a skymetal rod.

She glanced down at the bulge in my kilt, her

pale cheeks reddening, and looked away again. It took an effort to restrain a laugh at her shyness, but I didn't think she would appreciate the humor. Taking her chin between thumb and forefinger, I turned her head gently until we looked each other in the eyes.

"Will you behave yourself now? I do not want you eaten by animals."

"What do you care?" Victoria's retort stung. "I'm just your prisoner."

"A prisoner who has no value in the bellies of a kzor pack." The noises of the camp stilled around the tent, the Zrin who hadn't taken up the hunt hearing our raised voices and paying attention. I cursed. There was little space and no privacy in a warband's camp.

"Listen to me," I said, trying to keep my voice low but still stern. "I do not want you killed, so *stay where I put you*. If anyone sees you try to escape again, they *will* kill you. You can at least wait for a safer moment to escape if you must run away."

Victoria's lips twisted, her expression meaning-less to me. Amused? Angry? Frightened? It could be anything. Why didn't humans have ssavs? It would be so much easier to understand them if they did. But in the end she nodded agreement.

It did little to inspire confidence in her, of course.

She'd already shown she would lie for a chance to escape, but this was the best I'd get.

"Good. Now stay here while I send runners to call off the search for you."

She spoke a word I didn't know, but I recognized a curse when I heard one. Let her curse as long as she obeyed me.

Leaving the tent, I whistled for Sorcha and Kyrix. The two zsinz bounded over, Kyrix excited from the fighting, Sorcha looking hopeful, as though I might have another pack of kzor in the tent to give her as a treat.

"I wish I could oblige, girl. Next time you'll get to hunt and Kyrix will stay back with me."

Neither seemed thrilled with that promise, but it was all I had to offer them for now. Setting them to guard the tent, I called for runners to tell the other hunting parties of my success.

No sooner had I sent the runners off than Krosak appeared at my side. I shook my head, wondering where he'd been hiding and knowing it was futile to ask.

"I see you've caught your human, Lord," he said, rubbing his hands together. His ssav twisted and curled, white and purple mixing, and I watched him warily.

"I have. What of it?"

"Well now, I heard you sent runners for the other searchers," he said, leaning in close and speaking softly. "It will be some time before they return, though."

"If there's something you mean to say, say it," I snarled at my subordinate. Whatever it was, he knew I wouldn't like it, or he wouldn't hesitate to speak up.

On his ssav, colors twisted and shifted, and he glanced back at my tent. I gritted my teeth, drew up every ounce of calm, and braced myself to control my temper. *Deep breaths,* I told myself.

"Well, Lord," Krosak said, then faltered. Took a deep breath of his own and continued. "Lord, I do not know your plan, and I don't need to. What you intend to do with the human is your business, but... by the law, she must die."

He trailed off again, and I frowned at him. "Nonsense. I haven't brought her back here to kill her. If I wanted her dead, the forest would have obliged."

Despite my objection, his words sank into my heart like a dagger made of ice. It wasn't as though he was wrong, now that I thought about it. Those who went back on their surrender were to be slain as honorless scavengers. I'd made that law myself, and for good reason. Together with my promise to spare those who surrendered, it worked to keep conquered settlements in line while I looted them. That, in turn, made looting them easier and meant I didn't need to be brutal with them.

Now Krosak threw that back in my face, applying it to my captive. I snarled and Krosak stepped back, his hands spread and head bowed. For a moment I thought I'd lose control of my anger, but I caught hold of it and restrained myself.

"Getting the wisdom she carries back to our people is the entire reason for this raid," I ground out. "We've spent time, effort, resources we can't replace, and now you want to just slit her throat like she's nothing?"

"No, sire, no!" Krosak protested, shaking his head and backing away. "Please, I don't want her dead either! I have a better idea."

"So stop talking around it and *tell* me before I twist your head from your shoulders."

Keeping my voice down wasn't easy, and we were attracting attention that neither of us wanted. Krosak stepped closer and lowered his voice to a whisper.

"Sire, let us take her out into the forest together. You tell everyone you've sent me ahead to spread news of our victories and that you've slain her according to the law, I'll take her back with me and keep her hidden until I can bring her to you unseen."

That might even work. Or rather, it might solve one problem, but it would leave me with another. Krosak was my follower, yes, but one of the perils of claiming a throne is that you can never be sure who has your back and who wants to stick a blade in it.

Krosak was too cowardly to challenge me for leadership, but his plan would give him leverage against me. If he revealed that I'd spared Victoria and hidden her away, no one would trust my leadership and my power would melt away. Greed showed on his ssav, displaying his intentions. This wasn't loyalty, this was a power play, and I would not allow Victoria to become a bargaining chip.

"No." I answered with a single, flat, harsh refusal that should have made him back off. For once, Krosak showed some spine, pressing on into the face of my anger.

"But sire, you *can't* risk her life—"

Perhaps, if Krosak had explained his plan better, events would have unfolded differently. If he'd spoken as a friend, if he'd avoided telling me what I could and couldn't do, if he hadn't pushed the thought of Victoria's *death* into my mind, who knows what might have happened? Though not all the blame was his — had *I* been more receptive, less wound up with tension, I might have handled his defiance better. As it was, I reacted before my brain caught up with my body.

My hand hurt. Krosak sat on the ground, blood running from a split lip and eyes wide. I didn't remember hitting him, or even deciding to hit him, but here we were. Around the camp, those warriors not out on the hunt grabbed their weapons and eyed each other. A fight between leaders would spread fast as warriors chose sides, and no matter who won, too many Zrin would die.

That alone should have stopped me, but the fury welling up inside me set my blood aflame and demanded violence. Stepping forward, I grabbed Krosak's tail in mid-swing, his attack so obvious it gave me all the time I needed. A swift pull flipped him onto his face, and a hard kick to the ribs put a stop to his struggles.

"No one touches the human," I said. In a more cautious mood, I'd have kept my voice low to avoid embarrassing him in front of his warriors. Not now. Today, my fury had control and my voice rose. "You will not harm her, touch her, or do *anything* to her without my permission, nor will anyone else. If anything happens to her, Krosak, I will hold you responsible — you had better make *certain* she is safe. She is mine, and I will deal with her. Do you understand?"

Krosak wasn't a complete coward. He snarled and struggled, kicking backward with claws that would disembowel me if he connected. But he lay face down and I had his tail in my hands. Even a skilled warrior would have had trouble landing a hit.

Finally, he relented and stopped moving. "Yes Sire. I will obey. I don't understand, but I don't have to, I'll do as you command."

More defiance than I'd expected from him. To my surprise, I admired that — it meant I'd need to watch him, but it also raised my respect for him. My second in command was no longer a complete pushover, it seemed. I dropped his tail and stepped back out of range, just in case, but he rolled to his feet rather than attack me. All around us, a collective sigh of relief from the Zrin watching our confrontation. No one here *wanted* a fight, after all. At best, it meant killing allies. At worst, the horde might fracture into warring factions, an end to my vision of a united people.

To fend off any lasting feuds, I made a show of embracing Krosak, clapping him on the back and making it clear to our audience that we were firm friends once more. I regretted the time it kept me away from Victoria, but it had to be done to keep her safe as much as anything. "Come, Krosak, let us eat together and speak of the future."

All smiles, none of them reaching his eyes or his ssav, he clasped my arm and we set out to do damage control.

WHEN I RETURNED, washed and in fresh clothes, I had my emotions under control. More control, anyway. I couldn't say more than that, not when I didn't understand why I was on edge.

My two zsinz companions waited outside my tent where I'd left them, making sure Victoria stayed there too. Not likely to be needed, but I would take no chances with her, and they'd keep away other Zrin, too. That might be more important.

I threw Kyrix and Sorcha a couple of bones to repay their diligence and let them off duty. No need for my companions to stay up all night just because I planned to.

Victoria looked up as I pushed aside the leather

door-hanging, her face reddening. "Don't you know how to knock?"

Her voice held the snap of command, and her eyes flashed. Such fire, such strength — after all she'd been through tonight, she still defied me. Both annoying and impressive. My own simmering anger rose in response, and that wasn't all that rose.

"Watch your tone," I snapped, doing my best to ignoring the hardening under my kilt. "You are my prisoner."

Her wordless sigh wasn't one of fear, I thought, though it stayed hard to read her. I'd guess anger, frustration, perhaps amusement — but not a touch of fear. Why not? I knew I wouldn't harm her, but why would she so feel confident? She ought to be terrified, but I saw no sign of that in her now.

Only one way to find out. "You are sure of yourself for someone who tried to escape and failed. Why do you not fear me?"

Perhaps it was the directness of my question, but Victoria blinked in surprise as though she'd never imagined I could be interested in her feelings. For some reason, that made me more sad than angry.

Awkward silence stretched between us like the desert beyond the mountains, uncrossable and deadly.

Eventually, Victoria found her voice, shoulders stiffening as she made herself answer my question. "What's the point of being afraid when I'm already dead? Maybe you'll kill me for trying to escape, maybe not, but eventually you'll kill me. Might as well not worry about it."

Her words, so matter of fact and emotionless, stabbed my heart like a dagger made of ice. "I don't intend to kill you. More likely, you will run off into danger and get yourself killed. If I hadn't found you, it would have already happened!"

"And if you hadn't kidnapped me in the first place, I wouldn't have been in danger at all." Her retort stung. "You wrenched me from my home, out into the jungle. You can't blame me for trying to get back to the Vale."

"I'm not blaming you, human," I said, struggling to keep calm. I could only imagine what my ssav looked like, but she didn't react — perhaps because she didn't know how to read it. "But you ran off without any idea of how to survive. You would have gotten yourself killed, and then how would I interpret the human wisdom?"

That wasn't one tenth of the reason I wanted to keep her safe and sound, but I didn't understand the rest of my feelings well enough to express them.

Victoria looked at me, eyes narrow and hands on her hips, lips pressed together.

"I'm sure you could find someone else to explain better than I can," she said eventually. "I have no idea how to make a laser rifle or even refine steel. For that you'd want an engineer."

There were several words I didn't grasp in that sentence, but the gist was clear. I snorted. "Worthless trinkets don't concern me. It's clear from a glance that building your 'lasers' would take years to master, if not lifetimes. No Zrin I've spoken to even recognizes the *materials*, let alone how to use them. But you, Victoria, you hold the real magic of your people."

It wasn't easy to ignore the cute little furrow in her brow as she tried to puzzle out what I wanted. Or perhaps it was a sign that she found me as distracting as I did her. It took a heroic effort on my part to resist the urge to leap at her, claim her, take her as we both desired.

"If you're not looking for weapons, what magic are you after?" she asked eventually, breath catching. She leaned in towards me, tongue darting out to moisten her lips, and my heart raced. This was neither the time nor the place for such feelings, though, and I refused to respond to them. Focusing on her question, I explained what I needed from her.

As opposed to what I *wanted.* Every second I spent with her drained my self-control, led me closer to my snapping point.

"The magic of command," I answered. "Your humans, they work as one. No constant threat of violence, no one questioning your every decision. You can command those you never meet, even. *This* is the magic I want to learn, this art of controlling more people than you can keep under your gaze at all times."

She blinked at that. "Oh. That's... not what I expected."

I couldn't help laughing. "You expected me to want super weapons? Feh. What use is a laser against a warlord's ego? Some armors are impossible to penetrate."

"I'm not arguing, but a lot of guys don't agree," my captive said with a shrug and a grin. "Most of the men I've met would go for the new weapon and wouldn't give a fuck if it was practical."

"Many would," I agreed. "Many are fools, and insecure fools at that. I don't need a prop to show my potency."

Victoria muttered something under her breath,

cheeks reddening, before turning her gaze away. She tugged at her collar and took a deep breath. "What makes you think I can help you with that?"

"Do not play the fool, it does not suit you," I said, stepping closer. The tent wasn't large enough to give her space to retreat into and she stopped, backed into a corner. Her breathing fast, eyes wide, cheeks redder than before, there was still no fear in her. Nerves, yes, but not fear.

"You are the commander of the humans here," I continued, fighting to keep myself from pouncing. "You kept order, but you are not a warrior. I know you have this magic, and you will share its secret with me."

I'd prepared myself for many outcomes to my demands. None of them involved laughter, so Victoria took me by surprise. She doubled over, arms wrapped around her gut as I watched in confusion and annoyance.

"Sorry," she said, gasping for breath. "You think that staying in charge is a *magic trick*? That I have a way to make it *easy*?"

"Not easy," I said. "I don't fear hard work. What I need is some way to do it at all."

It took another couple of heaving breaths for Victoria to regain control of herself. Tears stained her cheeks and her body shuddered, but it was her eyes, sparkling with joy, that caught my attention. That drew me forward until I towered over her. Warmth radiated from her, inviting and enticing me, and she leaned in toward me. The powerful magnetism affected her as much as it did me, leaving the two of us on the verge of falling into each other. It drowned out all other needs. Sleep? Hunger? Conquest? These had no meaning against the call of Victoria's body and mind and soul.

The sharp noise of a tail striking muddy ground outside the tent brought me spinning round, the spell broken. Teeth bared, hand on my knife, I tore the heavy curtain aside, ready to gut whoever dared disturb us.

It was Krosak, of course, shifting his weight from side to side as he waited for me to emerge. After our last interaction, I hadn't expected him to seek me out for a few days at least — whatever brought him here was something that worried him more than my temper. I took a moment to calm down, settling my breathing and taking my hand from my blade. "What news do you bring?"

Killing a messenger would be a great way to ensure I never got another message. Tempting as that sometimes was, I decided against it and let go of my anger as he told me what was so important that he'd interrupted me.

"Lord, the hunting parties are back," he said. "They are not happy to have wasted the night out there and are grumbling about wanting to get back to their families. I came at once to tell you."

More trouble, less rest, and another chance for the horde to come undone. Keeping all the chieftains pointed in the same direction was work that never ended, and why I needed human leadership magic.

"I will come and smooth their ruffled fur," I said, grudging the need to leave Victoria. Perhaps it was for the best, though. A meaningful conversation should wait until we got home and I could show her the issues I faced. "Tomorrow we continue the march."

8

VICTORIA

I'd hardly gotten a wink of sleep before being rudely reawakened at dawn to continue the trek away from the Vale, from home, from safety. Tzaron hadn't returned to his tent all night, and he didn't summon me in the morning — two of his warriors came to fetch me instead, hurrying me out of the luxurious furs and into the damp forest.

The dawn itself was a disappointment, the rising sun hidden by the ongoing storm. A faint lightening of the sky through thick clouds, a jungle canopy, and pouring rain was all the change I saw, but it was enough. Enough to watch the Zrin pack up their things with a surprising speed, silent and disciplined.

The Zrin guards dragged me to Tzaron's side as he directed his own troops. My heart fluttered at the sight of him, standing tall and proud, his confident gestures directing an army that moved as one. It wasn't just his physique that drew me to him.

Stupid body, I thought, *I don't need some kind of Stockholm Syndrome crush on the asshole who kidnapped me.* Trying to control that was futile, though — I saw him and melted, a warm tingle running across my skin, my teeth catching my lip. The night before, when he'd trapped me in the tent, he could have done anything to me, and I'd have gone along with it. Anything at all. That kind of connection was dangerous, and I resolved to be on guard against it in future. I wasn't going to throw myself at the first tyrant to kidnap me; I had *some* standards.

"Victoria," Tzaron said, and my resolve blew away as soon as I heard my name in his deep voice. "You will stay with me as we travel."

I tried to find my anger, a solid bulwark against attraction, but my mind was too busy with that giant hunk of perfect muscle and wondering what, exactly, went on under his kilt. Not professional, I know, but my mind's eye stayed locked on him, undressing him, extrapolating the curves I saw.

"Worried I'll run away again?" I asked, pulling my gaze up with a herculean effort. Tzaron's lips pulled back in a grin, baring razor-sharp, pointed teeth. My own teeth sank into my lower lip and while I didn't understand why, my mind fixed on the idea of those teeth sinking into my shoulder as something else sank deep into my—

Shut up, brain. A tremor ran through my body, an electric tingle playing through my nerves. My pussy knew what she wanted and wasn't about to let my brain forget it. Fighting a losing battle for control, my brain resorted to snark.

"I know you are not so foolish," the tyrant rumbled, his voice emphatically *not helping* my internal battle. "You could not find your way home last night, and your chances only go down from there. But there are dangers on the road as well, and I won't have you walking into them. You are far too valuable."

"Shows what you know," I muttered under my breath. "I can't teach you our 'magic' without far better tools than I have."

"Then we will simply have to gather the tools you need."

Of course he heard me. Damn it. Resolving to

keep my internal dialogue *internal* from now on, I glared at him.

"You mean steal them."

"If you like." Tzaron shrugged and shook his head. "Call it what you will. You shall have your tools, and I will have my magic. But first, we must get you home."

With that, he lifted his pack, hissed a command to the Zrin around him, and set off at a brisk march. The Zrin commanders passed on the command, and soon the whole warband was on the move behind him — and me.

My thigh muscles burned almost as soon as we set out, last night's efforts taking their toll. It was hard enough to put one foot in front of the other, but with the Zrins' long strides, I had to jog to keep pace with Tzaron.

Despite having slept no longer than I had, he was annoyingly active. I couldn't complain, all I had to carry was the satchel with the datastore full of whatever Vassily had saved onto it. For its small size it was heavy, but nothing compared to the packs the Zrin all carried. Tzaron led by example there — and if anything, his pack looked heavier than most.

None of that slowed him in the slightest. I clenched my jaw, redoubling my efforts to keep up.

After what felt like a decade of marching through the forest (though Catula was quick to tell me it had only been a couple of hours), the Zrin stopped for a break at the banks of a stream. Swollen with rain running down from the mountains, the stream ran swift and cool, and I collapsed onto a rock beside it, my arm trembling with exhaustion as I reached down for the water. While they drank and refilled their water skins, all I could manage was to whimper and weakly splash my face. The icy water felt like life itself.

Tzaron looked down at me, surprising me with the lack of humor in his eyes. I'd expected amusement at my weakness, but his strange, alien eyes were shadowed with concern as he crouched. Beyond him, his two pet tengers lowered their tentacled faces to the water to drink. All the other Zrin gave them a wide berth, leaving us with some privacy in the midst of the horde.

Without a word, Tzaron reached down to the stream and lifted a cupped hand full of water to my lips. I couldn't care about dignity, not when my every muscle burned, and I felt like I hadn't drunk in a week.

The second time he brought his hand to my lips, he held me back, forcing me to drink slowly.

"Not too fast, or you will only feel worse," he said. "You are not strong enough for this journey."

"No fucking shit," I gasped, throat raw. "Does that mean you'll send me home, then?"

His booming laugh sent birds scattering from the trees and for just a second I saw his face clear of artifice and control. The harshness of his features softened, his smile was easy and honest, and the light in his eyes warmed.

"That wasn't a joke," I said, trying again to hold on to my anger. It was slipping in the face of his transformation. Seeing that my captor had a sense of humor made me feel safer around him.

Safer, not safe. There was and would always be an edge of threat to him, I realized — and with that realization came another. I didn't want him to be entirely safe. The danger was part of the attraction.

My cheeks burned when he brought another handful of water to my lips and despite the ache in every muscle, I felt a familiar, unwelcome, wonderful tingling running through me. Finding my strength, I pulled away and sat up, the cool rock under me and the rough, spongy bark of an alien tree at my back. I focused on those sensations to distract myself from the effect Tzaron had on me.

It *sort of* worked. A bit.

"I can't go on like this," I told him, hoping that he'd see the truth of that — and not just abandon me here, but give me an escort home or something.

He nodded, giving me a flash of hope. "It seems you are right. Humans and Zrin are different in so many ways."

I thought of marathon runners, and their inspiration, Pheidippides running across Greece for a day and a half to deliver a message to the Spartans. *Humans* can keep up this pace. At least some of us could — but despite my morning jogs, I didn't have the stamina.

Great, now I'm comparing myself to a half-remembered Athenian from three thousand years ago and failing that test.

"If you keep up this pace, it'll kill me," I said, pulling my mind back on track with an effort.

Tzaron dropped to the floor beside me, a graceful and silent movement that annoyed me more than it impressed. His legs weren't tired, weren't burning with effort. No, he was as fresh as the morning dew, while I lay panting and red-faced beside him.

"Your death is unacceptable," the alien warlord

said, as though that settled the matter. I wasn't allowed to die, he said so. I bristled but didn't object — it worked in my favor.

"Then you have to let me go. There's no alternative. If you keep going as we are, I won't make it to nightfall. Slow down for me, and you won't get far enough to avoid the Vale's militia once the storm stops. If you take me back, I swear we won't come looking for revenge. We'll leave you alone as long as you leave us alone."

His grin widened, eyes sparkling, but he didn't actually laugh. "Is that so?"

I nodded firmly. Tzaron shook his head, looking around at his warriors. They took turns to drink from the stream, with those who'd already drunk standing back to guard the rest from the dangers of the jungle all around us.

The different units (gangs? Packs?) had less coordination than I'd expected from Tzaron's army. Their officers kept having to separate Zrin before a fight got serious, and the officers kept looking daggers at each other too. They'd fought together well, but the strain was showing now. Even Tzaron would have trouble getting them to agree to a slow march on my account.

"You are counting on my Zrin lacking patience,"

he said, startling me with the accuracy of his assessment. "And you are not wrong to do so. But you neglect a detail — that is precisely why you are so valuable to us, even if the others don't recognize it."

"It hardly matters. No matter how valuable I am, if I die before I reach your base, I'm useless to you. You may as well send me home."

Tzaron's grin sent a shiver through me, mixing pleasure and dread. He didn't look concerned by the situation, which meant he was one step ahead. Not that he felt the need to enlighten me, the arrogant fucker. Instead, he lifted his pack, swinging it over his shoulders as though it weighed nothing. Around him, other Zrin took the hint and assembled their own gear.

"Why do you carry so much if you're in charge?" The question escaped before I thought about it or I'd never have asked it. I didn't want to know more, I wanted to get away, but somehow the question slipped through.

"Ha! How long do you think I'd be in charge if I didn't face the same hardships as my Zrin?" He sounded genuinely amused by my naïveté. "Better that they know I, too, am a warrior. Not some general hiding behind his troops, but doing the work they do, fighting beside them, carrying my share of the burden. Or sometimes more than my share."

With that, he bent over me and grabbed hold. I opened my mouth to protest, but all that emerged was a low moan as he lifted me from my feet. Strong fingers took hold through my clothes, digging into flesh, and my body ached at the thought of them touching bare skin. What would they feel like? Rough, I thought, but tender...

The enjoyable fantasy vanished as he whistled for his monstrous pets and unceremoniously dumped me onto one's back. The creature let out a plaintive meow and he chuckled, saying something I didn't follow.

"Wait, you can't—" That was as far as I got before the tenger bounded off at terrifyingly high speed, bounding over the swollen stream and into the jungle beyond.

THE NEXT FEW days were hell. Don't ask me how many, I lost count. If you've ever clung to the back of a deadly predator day after day, you'll understand. If you haven't had the experience, then for god's sake don't try it! The tengers were fast, uncomfortable rides, and I spent each day hanging on for dear life.

Whenever we paused, it took me the whole break to recover my breath, eat or drink, and curse out Tzaron for dragging me along on this hellish journey. He took that in good humor, which just made him more infuriating.

The nights were easier. Exhausted, I fell into a deep sleep as soon as my head hit the ground. Waking was another matter. Stiff and sore, my eyes opened as the Zrin around me ate and got ready for another day's grueling run. Every time I woke wrapped up in a blanket, cozy and warm — but that did nothing to help with the aching muscles that came from lying on the cold, hard ground.

And then there were the dreams. Only faint shadows of them remained when my eyes opened, the details vanishing like the morning dew. But some things were unmistakable. Every dream involved *him.* My Zrin captor Tzaron, chasing me endlessly, hunting me through the dark forest. When I put it that way, they sound like nightmares, but it was so much worse. I *enjoyed* the dreams. I woke from them with my body aching for his touch, wanting to see him, feel him, taste him. Every inch of my body wanted him in those moments of dawn before I put up my defenses.

After days of this torment, of being carried by him for painful days and dreaming of him for aching nights, the Zrin horde finally slowed to a walk in the middle of the afternoon. Tzaron set me down gently and grinned as I found my footing. "We arrive."

I could have burst into tears of relief at that, but I refused to give him the satisfaction. No more bouncing along for hours at a time? Fuck yes, I was grateful for that, but not to the man who'd dragged me into this.

"*Where* do we arrive? Where are we?" I looked around. We'd been climbing steadily towards the mountains as the jungle thinned out over the last few hours, and painfully bright patches of sky peaked through the canopy. Crashland's harsh sunlight was blinding after the storm and days in the deep forest, but aside from the bright light, nothing had changed.

And yet the Zrin around me seemed different, talking more and faster, laughing amongst themselves as they walked on.

Tzaron ignored my question, his broad grin promising me a surprise. Eyeing him warily, I followed — what else was I going to do? Running away here would be suicide.

The ground rose on either side of us, steeper and steeper, until even I couldn't miss that we'd entered a valley. Steep cliffs rose on both sides, rock walls rising high as the path we walked tended downward into the narrow pass. A flier would have to be directly overhead to see down to where we were, making it a cunning hideout for a raider's gang.

Or, as it turned out, a warlord's army. Tents in a dozen styles covered the ground at the bottom of the valley, Zrin bustling around them. There were more permanent structures, too — huts and a few stone buildings, with more under construction.

I bit my tongue to keep from showing my dismay. This valley wasn't as narrow as I'd thought, the high cliffs above and dark shadows below giving it a cramped feel. The camp held space for thousands of Zrin. Camp? No, this was a city, most of which happened to be mobile. And it was less than a week's travel from the Vale, at least for those who could run as fast as the Zrin.

Awed, I let my gaze roam over the settlement. Distinct districts melded into a single area of mixed architecture in shadow against the cliff face. Casting that shadow was a very familiar shape, and my mouth ran dry at the sight of it.

The *Wandering Star* had carried colony pods of all sizes. I'd ridden in one of the three biggest, intended as central hubs for our colony once we arrived on Arcadia.

Instead, I'd woken on Crashland to find the pods scattered across the planet. The fate of the other two mega-pods remained a mystery — until now. One of them stuck out of the ground at an angle, covered by a partial collapse of the cliff above. Its poor autopilot had done its best to control the approach, and the valley floor was a blackened desert where fusion jets had burned away plants and melted soil and rock into one flat surface. That must have slowed the descent since the pod was in one piece, but it hadn't done enough for a safe landing.

If Tzaron and his warriors had access to a mega-pod, then the knowledge I carried would be more useful to them than I'd thought. The industrial makers aboard were capable of 3d-printing spare parts for almost any human technology, given the raw materials.

Tzaron's hand landed on my shoulder, dragging me back to my immediate surroundings. All around us the warband gathered, impatient to get to the city below. I didn't blame them — I wanted to be home, too, but I had much further to go.

"What is this place?" I asked, shaking my head as though that would make the mirage disappear. Tzaron beamed with pride.

"We call it Hzirhu-Sza. That would be New City in the language of the Sky Gods. A city that I built from my conquests and the tribes I bent to my will. The seat of my empire, from which I shall drag the Zrin into the world of civilization."

That was the most he'd spoken of his plans. I swallowed, awed by the scale of them. *Time to revise my opinion. Tzaron may be a warlord; but there's nothing petty about this.*

"I must go ahead now," he continued, and I struggled to focus on his words. "There is a ritual to returning victorious."

"And it doesn't involve you having a human woman scampering after you, I suppose?"

He laughed at that, but there was an edge to it, and he didn't smile. "No. As much as I would like it to, it does not, and I can only flout tradition so far."

What little humor he had drained from his voice by the end of his reply, his voice going cold enough to make me shiver. Tzaron didn't intend to leave those traditions untouched. He wanted to reshape his society around him, and I didn't think Zrin culture stood a chance against him.

"Krosak here will guide you safely to the palace." Tzaron indicated another Zrin, shorter and with a furtive look to him. It was his eyes, darting everywhere and never settling, that made me suspicious of him. But it wasn't as though I had a choice. Tzaron trusted him and he'd know better than I did, so rather than arguing I just nodded. Tzaron strode off to the head of the column, leaving me with Krosak.

"You stay by me, yes?" His voice was exactly what I'd expected. Weaselly and low, the voice of a low-grade conman or a child trying to get out of trouble without technically lying about what happened to their homework. Perhaps I read him wrong. I had so little experience with his species, but my first impression was not good.

"Yes," I answered, because what else could I say? An unfaithful bodyguard was still better than being alone in this seething mass of alien warriors.

Making our way to the pass, I saw for the first time how many warriors Tzaron had brought with him on this raid. Hundreds of Zrin jostled for position behind their leaders and following them down a road carved into the cliff side. As we walked down it into the valley, I looked to my right and saw the drop, a long fall onto broken rocks. That made this place defensible, at least against other Zrin. If Torran and the militia got here with their lasers, the defenders would find themselves trapped at the bottom of this cleft in the mountainside.

Unless I showed them how to use the mega-pod's armory. I shivered, and not just because of the sudden chill as the shadow of the mountains fell across me. *I'll just have to make sure that doesn't happen.*

A Zrin, impatient to reach his home, shoved me aside I realized I'd slowed almost to a stop, gawping at this hidden city. Krosak grabbed my assailant by the arm, hissing savagely and proving himself to be a better protector than I'd expected.

Probably afraid of Tzaron rather than protective of me, but I'd take it. The other Zrin backed off hurriedly, and Krosak urged me down the path. Zrin pushed past us, eager to be home at last. As much as I tried, I couldn't keep up with them. Even with Krosak shielding me from the worst of the jostling, I was soon disoriented and struggling.

My focus entirely on the path, on getting to the city, on *please god* getting some actual rest, I stopped paying attention to the Zrin around me, assuming Krosak would keep me safe. A stupid mistake, one I wouldn't have made if exhaustion and shock hadn't overwhelmed my brain. That's always when things go wrong.

"So, you are the human our leader fusses over," someone said beside me. I looked left to see a Zrin I didn't know, though I recognized that awful grin on his face. I'd seen it before, countless times, on men who didn't think of women as people. A red flag on a dating site, a deadly danger in person.

He was tall, taller even than Tzaron, and scars cut across his face. Broad shouldered, bulky, the Zrin was a solid lump of muscle that ought to make the world shake with every step. He lacked any of Tzaron's grace and poise. Instead, he radiated a brutal menace that had none of the appeal Tzaron did.

I glanced around, looking for Krosak, but he wouldn't help me this time. Still close-by, he carefully had his back to us, deep in conversation with another Zrin. His alibi, I supposed, an explanation he could offer Tzaron for why he didn't see whatever was about to happen to me. A coward after all, though I didn't think it mattered. There were at least half a dozen hostile Zrin around us, and no amount of bravery on Krosak's part would keep them from doing what they wanted.

"Don't see why," another Zrin hissed, malice dripping from every syllable. His tail swiped at my legs and I barely avoided tripping over it. I did *not* want to find out if the Zrin behind me would stop or step aside and being trampled underfoot would be an awful way to die. The Zrin just chuckled, the others around him joining in.

Maybe it was tiredness, maybe I was just stupid, but it was only then that I realized how bad the situation was. The Zrin packed in around me tight, giving me no chance to escape them, and that wasn't an accident. They'd singled me out, cut me away from any potential allies, and none of them came from Tzaron's tribe. I'd learned that much about their clan symbols on the journey.

"What do you want?" I asked, keeping my head high and my voice level. "I am Tzaron's prisoner, he won't like it if anything happens to me."

Yeah, I hated invoking my captor's name, even in self-defense. But it was also a shield against them, whatever beef they had with me, and I had a very bad feeling that I needed a shield right now.

"That is the problem, yes," another Zrin answered. "You are his prisoner, but he carries you himself. He spends his time with you, not with the warriors he commands. We all rely on him having a clear head, and you fill it with szorc-droppings."

"It is not dignified," yet another chimed in. "You are not Zrin, not of the tribe. You are *nothing*. If he wishes to fuck his prisoner, fine, but he *cares*. That we can't allow."

My face glowed bright red. and I didn't pause to think about my words. "He hasn't! We haven't. I mean..."

My words trailed off. They wouldn't do anything to convince someone who didn't already believe me. The Zrin only looked angrier at my protests of innocence — they didn't want justice, they wanted blood, and defending myself only made things worse.

"You'll mess up everything," the Zrin on my right said, no trace of humor in his voice. "If he stays besotted with you, he will not take my daughter as his bride."

I brought my hands to my belt, unconsciously looking for a weapon. That was the tone of a man psyching himself up to violence and it didn't look like he had far to go. The others snarled at that, and I realized they didn't have shared goals. Or rather, they all wanted rid of me, but they had very different ideas about what happened next.

"I don't want to marry him, I don't want anything

from him," I tried to explain, my mouth dry. "He *kidnapped* me, and I just want to get home. Help me escape and I'll never bother you again."

A grim, humorless chuckle answered that. "What you want doesn't matter, human. You may not have noticed, but Tzaron's ssav hasn't shifted since he captured you. You are his taru-ma and he won't let you go, even if he doesn't realize that."

I blinked, dredging my memory. Taru-ma was what a Zrin called his mate, according to the files I'd read. His one true love, joined by fate. Which was a ridiculous superstition.

And yet, these Zrin took it seriously enough to kill me for it. *Fuck my luck.*

My trembling hands found nothing useful, and the Zrin crowded ever closer. They wouldn't be happy letting me go. Killing me would be easier and, from their point of view, smarter.

Letting them control our encounter would only end one way, so I tried to think of alternatives. There weren't many — shouting for help *might* attract attention, but even if it did, I didn't think the Zrin around us would help me. Bargaining was out, I had nothing to offer them. Begging for my life? The thought almost made me laugh, though that was mostly the stress.

All these options flashed through my mind at once, considered and then discarded between one footfall and the next. That only left one thing.

I tried to make the movement natural, swinging my arm a little further down, a little to the right — and snatching a blade from the nearest Zrin's belt. I didn't waste time posturing with it, instead stabbing to my left and throwing all my weight behind it.

That Zrin lord had impressive reflexes, twisting away from my attack. But in the tight crowd, he didn't have enough space to get out of the way, and the tip of the blade struck his shoulder.

Slid off a scale.

Caught between the next two and sunk in.

He cried out in shock as much as pain, his blood spraying across my face. The knife blade hit bone and stuck fast. I didn't waste time trying to remove it, grabbing another knife from his belt and spinning, slashing at the legs of the Zrin in front of me.

Something parted under the razor-sharp blade like a cable snapping, and the Zrin stumbled and fell. I leaped over him through the sudden gap in the ring of hostile Zrin, thinking I might have a hope of making it out of this death trap.

That thought ended when a tail struck my chest with bruising force, driving me back and to the ground beside my fallen foe. He snarled at me and I did my best to roll away, only to be stopped by a kick to the ribs as the other Zrin closed in around me.

Another tail knocked the knife out of my hand, and a hard kick rolled me onto my back, looking up into the bright blue sky and the faces of the Zrin surrounding me. As last views go, it could have been better.

9

TZARON

A nagging feeling of unease clung to me as I marched towards the gates of Hzirhu-Sza, Sorcha and Kyrix at my side. As leader, tradition demanded that I be the first to return, guiding my people home. Behind me came the leaders of the individual bands that followed me, and then the rest of the warband.

"Foolish custom, Lord," Heshra muttered behind me, supported by two of her scouts. "If the city's fallen, then they get the chance to kill you first."

I couldn't help smiling. She wasn't the type to let sentiment or tradition get in the way of a practical concern, and I wished I had the luxury to agree with her. Not yet, not while I was still establishing the new order. "Heshra, friend and companion, everyone who might take the city in our absence came with us on the raid. If I've misjudged things badly enough that someone else has taken it, I deserve to die."

Heshra made an unconvinced sound and stepped closer behind me. Sorcha tensed, but I knew Heshra better than that. If she intended me harm, she wouldn't act out in the open like this — it would be a silent knife under the ribs some night.

"Then I have bad news, Lord Tzaron. Some of those Zrin you wanted close are not." She hesitated, choosing her words carefully. "They've left their customary spots."

Glancing back, I saw that she was right. Gessar had left the position of honor to another, and that wasn't like him at all. Not unless he had an important matter deal with.

Others were missing too. Lesser leaders had more leeway — sometimes a commander would allow a subordinate who'd done well on a raid to have the honor of leading a warband home. But three at once? When no one had spoken of the great deeds of a lieutenant? I didn't believe that.

The obvious possibility was that they'd planned an ambush on the vanguard and didn't want to stand near me when the blade fell. I couldn't rule that out, but something didn't feel right about it.

Stopping was not an option, not with home *right there* and my warriors' packs full of loot. Oh, most would obey, but enough wouldn't to make me a laughingstock. In hardly any time I'd be past the gates and then I'd have the freedom to—

Something sharp dug into my heel, as though someone stabbed me with a handful of needles. It caused more surprise than pain, but it drew my attention even though it did me no harm. I turned my attention to whatever had attacked me.

Vicky's ghost-animal looked up at me, claws and teeth all digging into my skin. It looked weak, almost not there at all, a shadow where it had been a pool of darkness. My heart lurched at the sight — this thing existed to serve Vicky and seeing it here rather than at her side had to mean something was wrong. Badly wrong.

"Heshra, you have the honor of leading the troops home." The words left my throat before I'd considered them, and Heshra's look of awed horror would have been funny if I had time to focus on it.

"But, sire," she stammered. I didn't wait to hear her objections, shoving my way against the tide of warriors. I didn't dare slow and risk losing track of Victoria's spirit companion in the crowd.

A knot of action up ahead drew my attention. Brawls were common enough in a warband as large as mine, but this didn't look right. To the side of the marching troops, on a small outcropping above the stream running through the valley, six Zrin stood in a tight circle facing inward, kicking at someone huddled in the center. The ghost-pet rushed toward them like a black arrow.

I followed, my heart freezing solid as I saw a flash of red hair from their victim and knew for sure who it was. My run became a charge, and I didn't even try to identify Victoria's attackers. Who they were didn't matter, stopping them did. Victoria needed me, and I cursed myself for allowing tradition to keep me from her side.

The same noise that covered this brutal attack disguised my approach, and none of the attackers noticed me till I was in amongst them, clawing and tearing.

The first charge knocked my enemies back, two of them wounded, one fatally. Not enough. I stood over the fallen human and roared at them as they backed away in all directions. Even as angry as I was, l kept enough control not to follow them. I'd slay whoever I caught, yes, but I'd also give the other three an opening to kill Victoria.

"Traitors and cowards," I shouted, trying to watch all four of the retreating Zrin. Behind them, the column of warriors paused to watch the fight. A half-dozen Zrin kicking someone to death wasn't much to concern them, but when their warlord got involved, that promised entertainment worth pausing for.

My foes noticed that as well, and I saw them weigh the loss of face from retreating against the risks of fighting me. I took that moment to look at who I'd picked this fight with — *not* good news. Three of the survivors were warband leaders, and worse, one of them was Gessar. No surprise, but I'd hoped there was another explanation for his absence at the head of the column.

I bared my teeth, my tail whipping from side to side viciously. Slaying him might split my empire into warring factions, but he'd attacked Victoria and would die for that.

"Lord Tzaron," Gessar said, "we are neither cowards nor traitors, we work only for the good of our people."

He didn't shout, but he had a knack for public speaking, projecting his voice so all could hear. More and more of the Zrin passing by stopped to watch, making me curse under my breath. No way to settle this quietly then. So be it.

"Cowards to attack the human rather than come to me with your concerns," I said, my voice reverberating off the cliffs. Gessar wasn't the only one with such tricks. "Traitors because you would slay the one we need."

"We don't need her, Lord, not when you are here to guide us," Gessar said, his ssav twisting and turning as he felt his way through the lie. Fearful white faded, overtaken by orange and red and green to match the smile I wanted to tear off his face. "But she keeps you from us. Every day you spend time with her, she steals time from us and keeps you from your people. She is a witch, and we only hoped to save you from her clutches."

Every word sounded sincere. If I hadn't seen his ssav, he might have fooled me. But Gessar was no fool; he aimed his words at the Zrin gathered behind him, and they saw nothing of his ssav. They only heard his words, which sounded reasonable.

To my surprise, they had no impact on me at all. What he said had some merit, even if his ssav made it clear he was manipulating the truth. My human captive had her ghost companion, she refused to accept when she was beaten, and she had strange, forbidden knowledge. And some power drew me to spend time with her, away from my responsibilities and my warriors.

But I didn't believe it for a heartbeat. Victoria was my prey, mine alone, and no word of anyone else would turn me aside from her. *Now try to convince the others of that,* I thought. Their reaction was obvious — they'd say she'd cursed me, controlled me, made me blind to her wiles. It would give them a fresh excuse to kill her, that was all. I needed another approach.

"She is my kill," I snarled back. "I captured her, and I will keep her until her usefulness to the war is over. Anyone who would *steal* her death from me will die for it like the honorless szorc they are."

That resonated with the crowd too, and I left out the fact that I didn't intend to kill her. Let them come to that truth gradually. Right now, I'd prefer to avoid any more arguments that might turn deadly. Once Victoria was safe in my palace, I'd be able to be more forthright.

Such concerns of honesty didn't hold back Gessar, though. Matching eyes with me and keeping his air of false concern, he continued. "I fear, my Lord, that the human has bewitched you. Look to your ssav, Sire, her magic fools you into thinking she is your taru-ma. This female must die *now,* to free you of her influence."

Oh. A thousand clues clicked into place and my heart thumped. She was my mate. Of course she was my mate. And no wonder everyone had laughed when I'd pretended indifference — anyone close to me could see what I'd missed, that my ssav had frozen. The indignity of being told by my enemy stung like salt in a wound.

Who looks at their own ssav? This was a farce as old as time, hundreds of stories told of lovers who didn't know that they were mated until someone else told them. Stories that, until today, I'd thought funny but unlikely.

Now I starred in one. And, if I wasn't careful, it would end a tragedy.

Gessar was smart, perhaps too smart. In front of so many of my Zrin, he put me in a place where I'd either accept his words and lose authority to him or defy him. In which case the rumors that I was under Victoria's spell would spread like wildfire through the horde, undermining my authority.

Or we fought, and he had his chance to kill me.

"You call me a slave to magic?" I demanded, my voice reverberating across the horde. "You say that I am *weak?* We shall see about that, Gessar. Come forth and fight me, and I will show you I am no weakling."

Gessar's grin widened as silence spread through the valley. He'd known what I would choose, he'd relied on it. "With heavy heart I accept, Lord. May the Sky Gods free you of this curse."

With that, he stepped forward and straightened up to his full height, looming over me. Massive, muscle-bound, with arms like tree-trunks, Gessar was a mighty warrior indeed. Almost a head taller than me, and fast for his size, he'd be dangerous even if he didn't have his cronies at my back.

"You do not have to do this," I told him quietly. "You risk breaking the horde, just as we need to be strong together. I will overlook this if you back down now — you will have many chances for greater power."

His entire body trembled as he held back a laugh. "Tzaron, you are a magnificent warrior, but you think too much of the future. Your plans, ah what mighty dreams they are, but no more substance than a flake of snow. Grasp them and watch them vanish. No, I will take the power I can see over the illusion you offer."

There was no malice in his tone, just a clear, cold

grasp of the facts as he saw them. Saying it so bluntly meant he intended for me to die. Well, so be it — I wouldn't do him any favors either, not after his treatment of Victoria. We both nodded coldly to each other, braced ourselves, and charged.

10

VICTORIA

*W*as I dead yet? The pain hadn't stopped, the throbbing agony spreading through my entire body, making me feel sick and robbing my thoughts of their speed and clarity. But no new kicks landed, no fresh pain burned through my nervous system.

Can't be dead. Too noisy. I don't know why that thought was persuasive, but I forced my eyes open to tell whoever was making the noise to turn it down. Some of us were trying to rest in peace, you noisy fuckers.

Figures stood in front of me, and I tried to remember who they were. One, the huge and dangerous Zrin, I remembered vaguely. Yes, he'd been one of the Zrin kicking me — the memory brought a shudder and I turned away from it.

Though the other Zrin had his back to me, I recognized him instantly. *Tzaron.* There he stood, between me and harm. He might be my kidnapper, but he was protecting me. I didn't have to understand that to appreciate it.

My eyelids hung heavy as I slumped again, but before they closed, I watched Gessar pounce, Tzaron leaping to meet him in mid-air, as though this was some kind of superhero show.

MY EYES OPENED AGAIN. How long had they been shut? A second, an hour, a day? No idea. *That is not a good sign,* I told myself.

In front of me the two Zrin still fought, sections of the crowd cheering them each on. That gave me a name to put to that scarred face — Gessar. Despite my life being on the line, everything felt so distant and unconnected, like a vibrant, colorful painting reduced to black and white. The two almost seemed to dance rather than fight.

Until Gessar made a leap in my direction, striking at Tzaron as he went. In this blurred, slowed-down view, I saw Tzaron's choices. Simple and inescapable: he could dodge, avoid the onrushing attack, and leave me at Gessar's mercy for a moment. Or take the hit and stay between us, risking losing the fight to protect me.

Everything unfolded excruciatingly slowly, as though they were swimming through honey. Tzaron tensed, turned aside, sprang back out of his opponent's way. I didn't blame him for that — if he lost the fight, I'd die anyway. He might as well save himself, I reasoned without emotion, watching my death descend. I had just enough self-awareness to realize that this calm wasn't normal, was another bad sign.

Razor-sharp claws swung at my throat, and I told myself I should avoid them. But moving took so much energy, the air thick as molasses holding me in place for Gessar's fatal blow.

Which twisted out of the way as Tzaron pounced onto Gessar's back. The two hit the rocky ground just out of reach of me.

Time snapped into normal speed as I scrambled back, every nerve in my body protesting and my eyes on the fight before me. Gessar's tailspine embedded in Tzaron's stomach, a gruesome lesson in why you should never attack a Zrin from behind. Tzaron's claws tore into his enemy's shoulder, his other hand grabbing the tail and squeezing hard.

For a moment I thought he'd won despite the terrible wound, but Gessar was having none of it. A brutal twist flung Tzaron away, blood spraying, the tailspine doing more damage on the way out than it had on the way in. Tzaron got his own strike in as they separated, claws tearing into Gessar's tail, and the two bloodied warriors lashed out at each other with more anger than skill. Their brutal struggle brought them rolling closer and closer to the cliff's edge, a long fall to jagged rocks below. I tried to think of something to do, but my eyes drifted shut again.

SHOUTS of confusion and anger brought me back to consciousness, if I could call this washed-out state 'conscious'. The two other chieftains who'd attacked me ran in, aiming themselves at the dueling pair. The shouting came from the crowd behind them, some trying to rush forward, others holding them back, no one clear which side they were on. They'd keep themselves busy long enough to avoid getting involved in the fight.

Not the two leaders, though. And, injured as he was, Tzaron didn't stand a chance against three skilled opponents.

Why did *that* pull away the fog slowing my thoughts? Yes, if Tzaron died I'd soon follow, but the threat to me hadn't shaken off my paralysis before. Now, though, looking at death coming right for Tzaron, I felt a cold lump in my stomach and my mind kicked into overdrive trying to find a solution.

Physically stopping them wasn't possible. Even if I found the strength to stand, even if I reached them in time, I was no match for one of those Zrin, let alone both. Speaking? No real chance anyone would listen, not in time to save Tzaron.

My last idea was crazy, but it had the advantage that it might work. It *might*. "Catula?"

The black cat hologram shivered into existence in front of my face, cocked his head to the side, and meowed. Thank goodness — the wristband had taken a few hits when I raised my arms to protect myself. No time for relief now, though. "Catula, I need you to playback something, okay? Quickly."

A menu popped into existence above his head, listing all his stored recordings. As I scrolled through, I watched the fight from the corner of my eye. Tzaron, backed against the edge, faced three opponents and only the fact that they couldn't all reach him at once kept him from falling. But it was only a matter of time unless — *there!*

I tapped the recording, biting back a scream from the movement. Something in my arm wasn't right, but that was just another problem to put off until I had time to worry about it.

Count Catula opened his mouth wide and let out a high-pitched whistle loud enough to shake the cliffs. The Zrin army looked around, confused and trying to find the source of the sound. Behind them, I heard a commotion. Even the four fighting at the edge of the cliff paused.

An answering scream filled the air, and Zrin leaped aside to get out of the way as Tzaron's twin tengers burst through, summoned by my recording of his calls to them in the jungle. Seeing their master, they bounded toward him and the three attackers.

Gessar made one last attempt to shove Tzaron off the edge, but his companions panicked and tried to flee. Facing only one foe, Tzaron slipped to the side, avoiding Gessar's attack and striking back with a blow that felled him like a tree in a hurricane.

He had no chance of chasing down the fleeing warlords, but he didn't need to. His tengers had no difficulty intercepting them, venomous tentacles slapping them and bearing them to the ground. The crowd cheered and I lay back, exhausted.

I guess that worked, I thought, and let the dark take me.

THE NEXT TIME I opened my eyes I sighed with relief, looking up at the white ceramoplastic ceiling above. I'd never been so pleased to see the boring, practical material. It meant that the attack was just a nightmare. No alien warlord had dragged me into the jungle. I hadn't left the Vale at all.

I tried to pull back the blanket, but my arms refused to work and a stabbing pain shot through me, warning me not to push myself too hard. My mouth was too dry to curse, so I let myself fall back onto the soft, yielding, heavenly mattress in silence.

Something bothered me enough to keep me from sleeping, though I couldn't work out what. My brain full of cotton wool, I struggled to line up my thoughts. When that didn't work, I tried to list the things that weren't right.

1. This is not my room. It's too big, and it smells different.

2. It hurts to move, even a little.

3. I can't remember what happened last. Only the nightmare.

Oh crap, I'm in medbay, aren't I?

It made sense but said nothing about how I'd gotten there. Maybe trampled by the bigfur stampede? Or was that just part of the dream?

"Catula will know," I muttered, slurring my words. "What's the point of a companion who doesn't keep track of my injuries. Count?"

With a self-satisfied *meep,* the hologram fizzled into existence on my chest and looked down at me. Another good thing about holograms was that they could sit on your cracked ribs without hurting you.

"How long have I been out?"

Catula's eyes blazed green, projecting a timer into the air between us. Eighteen hours, thirty-two minutes, and some seconds. Okay, that had to be a bad sign, didn't it? Still, better than being an alien's prisoner, and the target of a murder attempt.

"Diagnosis?" I croaked. Catula meowed back, and the timer swapped out for a human silhouette colored to mark my injuries. I winced — that looked a lot worse than I'd thought, with several cracked ribs and serious bruising spread across my torso.

But at least I was in the Vale with civilized

medical technology, not in some iron-age shaman's care or whatever the Zrin had. I lay back again, looked at the ceiling, and grimaced. That was a good thing, but I felt an ache in my chest that had nothing to do with my injuries.

Don't be fucking ridiculous, you don't even like Tzaron. The thought of his name brought another pang of loss. I tried talking myself through it. *Come on, pull yourself together — yes, fine, you thought up the hottest man for a hundred light years, but he still kidnapped you.*

Whatever I told myself, though, my body wasn't listening. I warred with my emotions, helpless against the crashing waves of them, until I heard the door slide open.

"Oh thank god," I muttered, then raised my voice to a croak. "Doctor, what happened?"

"Speak Sky Tongue, human, not whatever that awful language is." The hissing, inhuman sound of a Zrin speaking Eskel made me forget my injuries and sit up to look at the newcomer.

Ah. It's the shaman after all, some distant part of me thought. All the relief I'd felt moments ago ran out of me like water from a dropped glass and I sank back, trying to come to terms with the idea that I really had been kidnapped by aliens.

There was a silver lining, though. Tzaron was real, and here. I swallowed, mouth and throat dry, and tried to ignore the tension running through my body at that. *Focus on recovering; right now I couldn't jump rope let alone jump him.*

"Water?" I croaked out, and an unfamiliar Zrin face appeared above me, grinning and offering me an earthenware cup full of something pungent. Not what I'd asked for, but I was in no position to make demands. When the Zrin touched it to my lips, I drank without thinking about it.

Thick, fruity, unpleasantly sweet — a flavor like nothing I'd ever tasted. I didn't care about the *taste*, though. I gulped down swallow after swallow until the Zrin pulled the cup away.

"Too fast. You must drink slowly."

I nodded, gasped, and turned my head to get a good look at the newcomer. Wise eyes set deep into a sharp face, hair tied back in a complicated braid, carrying herself with a professional air, she'd have looked like a doctor except for the bone charms dangling from her wrists and neck. She was slighter than the warriors I'd traveled with, though still muscular enough to be a deadly threat if she wanted to be.

The grin crept up on me, sneaking onto my face

without my permission. A *five-year-old* would be a deadly threat in my current condition.

"What happened?" I asked again, this time in Eskel. The Zrin woman shrugged.

"You think they tell me anything? Just because I'm the river that bears the knowledge of the Sky Gods back to them? You humans aren't bright, huh?" with strong, practiced hands she lifted me and shoved another cushion behind me, helping me sit up. "All I know is, Warlord Tzaron brought you back from a raid, furious about your wounds. He's holding a council to judge the Zrin responsible, but do I get to hear the full story? No I do not, because I have to check on *you.*"

"Uh, sorry?" I started. "I didn't mean to keep you out of anything."

"Of course you didn't." The Zrin worked on something in the far corner, and I raised my head to see. On one of the white ceramic counters, she'd set up something that looked like the wizard's laboratory out of some classic camp horror series, and it looked as though she was mixing up a witch's brew, grinding things up and pouring them into a bottle.

"What's in that?" I asked, knowing it was pointless. The Zrin names for the plants involved would be nothing like what we'd named them, and it wasn't as though I knew their properties even if I understood which plants she meant.

I'd asked, though, so I paid close attention to the answer, if only to be polite. It was as meaningless as I'd expected, but still soothing somehow, and I'd guessed right — full of passion for her interests, she'd talk about them at the slightest prompting. Her eyes shone as she told me details that meant nothing to me, gesturing expressively when her hands weren't holding equipment.

That enthusiasm was enough to boost me, too. Or was it something in the drink? It didn't matter. The important thing was that I could move a little if I was careful.

When she ran out of things to say about the medicine she looked sheepish, the patterns on her scales shifting to twisting strands of gray. I tried my best smile.

"Thank you for explaining, even if I can't understand half of it. My name is Victoria, by the way."

"Victoria." She tested the shape of the name in her mouth, repeated it a few more times, then nodded. "I am Zsatia."

She said it as though it was a name, so I nodded and greeted her as she rubbed the paste she'd prepared into my arm. The nagging ache of the bruises there subsided, replaced by a faint tingling numbness — I still had sensation there, but it was as though my arm was wrapped in cotton wool.

"I am supposed to tell our Glorious Ruler as soon as you wake, but Tzaron is holding court to judge your attackers. It promises a grand spectacle when he feeds them to his zsinz, and I shall miss it tending to your wounds." She checked my bruises with rough but careful hands as she spoke. "I would not pull him away from such important work, especially when you are weak and injured. There's no telling what his desires would lead to, if I leave you alone in a room together."

She chuckled, and my cheeks heated. I knew what she was thinking, and while I wanted to argue, she was right. Put me and Tzaron together in a room with a bed and I wouldn't bet on our self-control. Tzaron had been the one thing I'd missed when I thought my capture had been a nightmare, and the thought of him enveloping me in those strong blue arms made my heart beat faster.

But that wasn't the most important part of what she'd told me, just the part my brain fixed on first. The rest of it hit all at once and I swore, struggling to pull myself up from the bed. "I have to stop that trial."

I tried to sit up, only for Zsatia to push me back down into the mattress. "No. You need to rest, you need to sleep, and you certainly don't need to barge in on a sacred rite where the warlord doles out the justice of the tribe."

"You don't understand," I gasped, struggling. That would have been futile when I was at my best — in my current condition it was embarrassing.

"I don't need to *understand* a command to obey it. I understand my duty and that's enough."

She sounded calm and implacable. Appealing to her emotions wasn't going to get me anywhere. I needed an argument to get through to her and I cast about for one.

"Zsatia, Tzaron is judging the Zrin who attacked me," I tried. She didn't react, so I continued. "They are my foes too; shouldn't I be able to see them meet their fates? And Lord Tzaron did tell you to let him know as soon as I was awake — he might want me there, and if you don't tell him now, you might mess up his plans."

She tilted her head to the side, considering, then laughed. "You are good at arguing. Too good, you remind me of the doctor before me, the one who raised me to this cursed profession. Very well, I will help you to the great hall, but should your wounds take hold of you, it is not my doing."

"Yes, I'll take responsibility," I promised, swinging my legs over the edge of the bed as soon as she removed her hand from my chest. "We have to hurry."

My legs gave out as soon as I put weight on them, but Zsatia caught me on the way down, laughing again.

"Are you certain you want to risk this?" she asked, helping me get my balance. I nodded, doing my best not to tremble, and her mouth twitched into an odd smile. "In that case we'd better find something for you to wear."

I glanced down and yelped. Bad enough that I planned to interrupt a warlord at council, but I'd been about to do it *naked*.

My defeated foes knelt before me on the floor of the great hall. Great fires lit the chamber, smoke staining the off-white roof, and I wondered yet again how the builders of this amazing structure had managed to forget an opening to let the smoke out.

Somehow the Sky People were amazingly clever and unbelievably stupid at the same time.

Krosak listed the charges levied against the three Zrin facing my judgment. It was a long list, longer than it needed to be, but he'd pointed out that the more crimes we convicted them of, the less likely their warbands were to back them. It was a serious concern, especially in Gessar's case — his warband was strong, second only to mine, and if they rebelled as a group it would tear my horde apart.

Even if they didn't, I expected to face trouble. Feuds, reprisals, and warriors deciding to pursue their futures elsewhere — those were the problems I foresaw if things went well.

Beside Gessar knelt Lorssan and Eeiras, lesser leaders but not without influence. Both were bulky, unimaginative warriors in the old style, used to using force to take what they wanted. Little imagination, strong enough to keep their Zrin in line, too foolish to grasp beyond that.

And today I'd have to kill them both, probably exile their followers, and deal with the bad blood that brought me. Wonderful. I wanted to shout at them and find out why they'd behaved so stupidly, but I couldn't — not with the audience gathered at the chamber's edge, half-hidden by the smoke and shadows. Zrin from every band in my horde, here to witness justice being done.

Krosak's list of crimes ended with a flourish. Bravery in battle might not be his thing, but here in court he came alive, his voice rebounding from the strange walls of the chamber. It was easy to think of him as a bumbler and a coward, but that ignored the fact that he'd led his own warband, and here was how he'd done it. Even Gessar looked a little shaken at the litany of charges and the weight of the audience's glares.

Of course, Krosak had every reason to give his best performance. He was lucky not to be kneeling beside the accused and facing his own death sentence. Only the fact that he'd been helpless in the face of three warbands kept him from the fate that awaited these traitors.

I hissed my satisfaction, gripping the arms of my throne hard enough to leave marks on the solid metal. "Well, Gessar, have you any defense against these charges?"

There was fire in his eyes when he looked up to meet my gaze.

"I don't need one, because we all know that this 'trial' is nonsense," he hissed back. "If we wanted to obey laws, we'd have stayed with our tribes not taken our chances in the wild."

A rumble of approval from the half-seen audience. They liked that myth, many of them preferring it to remembering that their tribes exiled them for crimes they'd committed.

"The old laws were forced upon you by generations of ancestors," I said, firm but calm. "Many of them were unjust. Here, out in the wilds, we make our own laws — and you swore to follow mine when you joined this horde. If you regretted that choice, you were always free to leave."

His glare hardened, and the audience fell silent around us. Perhaps I'd defused that problem, but more than likely it would rear up again later. So be it. All I needed was for the situation not to explode *right now* when I killed this trio.

"Why argue?" Gessar said at last. "We both know that you've already decided my fate, so come kill me and stop yapping about it."

At least we agreed on something. I pulled myself from my throne and lifted the heavy-bladed executioner's sword that rested beside it. Little use in a fight, the weapon had one purpose only: separating a criminal's head from his body. It rested uncomfortably in my hands. I never liked the idea of killing someone unable to fight back, but these three had tried to slay Victoria. That thought hardened my resolve, and I tightened my grip on the sword's hilt as I walked toward my captured foes.

The other two cowered, but Gessar kept his eyes focused on me. Give him half a chance, and he'd make it a fight. I almost let him, but no. I refused to give him an opportunity to avoid the death his crimes deserved.

My sword weighed heavy in my hand as I wound up for the fatal blow. Gessar's face twisted into a snarl when I paused. "Do it, you coward. Kill me and make your own doom certain. You will follow me, and soon."

I don't know how I would have answered that. With the sword, perhaps, taking his head off. Before I could find out, a shout echoed through the hall.

"Stop!"

Every head turned toward the unexpected intrusion into the council, mine included. And there, in the doorway, stood Victoria. The surprise nearly made me drop my sword.

She looked majestic, marching into the hall wearing only a fine sheet of metal cloth wrapped around her to make a crude dress that left nothing to the imagination. Barefoot, she strode into the room, face set and hiding the pain that I saw in her eyes. Zsatia followed, giving me a helpless shrug. Though I wanted to be angry with her, I sympathized — getting Victoria to do as she was told wasn't easy.

"Victoria," I started, unsure what else to say. I needn't have worried. She switched to Sky Tongue and kept talking.

"No, Tzaron. You can't kill them." Her voice caught and she stumbled over her words, but she got her meaning across. "It's, it's a mistake. Will cause more harm than, than good."

"You cannot be serious," I said, the words bursting out before I could think of a more diplomatic reply. "They raised their hands against you, and for that crime they will die."

The rest of the chamber was silent, an aching silence almost as deafening as thunder. The audience looked at Victoria, eyes wide with horror that an outsider would burst in on our meeting like this, let alone to defend her attacker. I glanced at Gessar — his ssav writhed, ugly green-gray colors shifting and wrapping around his torso like some terrible constricting animal. His snarl of outrage completed the picture, and if Victoria had been in reach of a lunge, he'd have tried to kill her. Even with the spear at his back and certain death as a consequence.

He didn't want to die, but the prospect of being saved by his would-be victim was even less appealing. I'd feel the same way in his place, but I didn't need to worry about his feelings.

Victoria stepped forward, looking cool and composed, as though someone had sculpted the most beautiful woman in the world or the Sky above out of ice. Only her eyes, flicking from Zrin to Zrin showed that she knew the danger she'd walked into.

Too many of the Zrin here had reason to want her dead, and her trespass into the trial was cause enough.

"They have broken the laws I set," I said, trying to be gentle and to protect her. "The penalty is death, and I will not stay my hand."

Victoria looked down at the defendants silently, leaving the only sound the crackling of flames from the fires lighting the room. Despite the heat from the flames, she showed no sign of discomfort. A handful of heartbeats later, she spoke again.

"You are responsible for my safety, Lord Tzaron," she said without a trace of a stammer. She'd taken the time to think about what she was about to say, and my hands balled into fists out of sheer annoyance at what was coming. Sky Gods help me, she had a plan.

"When you took me captive, you promised I would be safe. But these men under your command tried to kill me and nearly succeeded."

"I saved you," I interrupted, but she waved that aside.

"It is your responsibility as their leader. To repay that failing, I ask for these Zrins' lives. Spare them and we're even."

She looked me straight in the eye as she spoke,

her gaze passionate and pleading. Around the chamber, Zrin muttered amongst themselves, some translating for those who spoke little of the Sky Tongue. The murmurs weren't easy to interpret, but overall, I judged them to be approving.

And more importantly, this was important to Victoria. Why she didn't want bloody vengeance I didn't know, but what did that really matter? Her point stood: she was the victim these villains attacked, she deserved to have a say in their fate.

Couldn't she have had a quiet *say?* The thought was unfair, and I knew it — here she was, fresh from her sickbed and wrapped in a sheet, and she'd barely arrived in time. There'd been no chance for her to speak to me in private.

Hiding my frustrated sigh, I turned back to Gessar and the others. It was some comfort to see them vibrating with a mix of hope, fear, and shame.

"Your lives are spared," I said. "You owe them to Victoria the human. Never forget the kindness she has shown you here and know that there will not be a repeat of this mercy."

Gessar's glare dispelled any hope that this ended here. No matter. Killing him would have had consequences too, and I'd never know which would be worse. His companions, though shamed by the manner of their rescue, accepted it more readily, bowing low to Victoria and backing away into the crowd. As soon as they reached their own warbands, they turned and left as fast as their legs would take them.

Unlike his companions, Gessar was not one to bow. Standing tall, he sneered at me and turned his back, pushing through the crowd without a look behind him. The Zrin around him grumbled, some happy with this outcome, others less so. This would take time and work to sort out.

Right now, I had other things on my mind.

12

VICTORIA

*T*he trio of murderous warlords left, their followers gathering around them. None looked grateful to me for saving their lives, but their gratitude wasn't why I'd done this.

For the first time I took my eyes off the assembled aliens, looking at the room I'd stepped into. Perspective shifted, and I realized it was the rec room, twin to the one back at the Vale. Though the shape was the same, the Zrin had modified this one to suit themselves, lighting fires, hanging tapestries on the walls and by Tzaron's throne, it was an impressive space. Back at the Vale settlement we used our mega-pod's rec room for meetings too, but we hadn't hung the walls with furs or stained the roof with smoke.

I kept my eyes on my surroundings, trying not to think about the danger I'd thrown myself into. Tzaron's gaze burned into me, and I knew that if I looked at him, I'd be lost. Instead, I looked at his raised throne, looming over the room and making me wish I'd chaired the council from a seat like that back in the Vale. If that hadn't shut up the other representatives, Sorcha and Kyrix would have. The pair of zsinz flanked Tzaron's throne, heavy chains binding them to it, and every other Zrin gave them a wide berth.

At last the remaining Zrin were gone, Zsatia hissing a whisper as she passed.

"Don't get yourself back into my care, human. I've spent enough time patching you up already."

I *think* that was meant as a friendly jab.

At last, the room emptied down to just me and Tzaron. Still, I didn't dare look at him, just pulled the sheet tighter around me.

"Why did you make me spare them?" Tzaron said after about ten thousand years of silence. "They would have killed you."

The question brought my head round to stare at him, torn between anger and shock. I settled on confusion.

"Why? You ought to know that, Tzaron. It's the

same reason you wanted to kill them. I was protecting you." Though why I'd risked my life to do that, I didn't know.

"Why in the Sunless Depths would you think I needed your protection?"

"Because, dumbass, you were going to get yourself killed." I glared at him as I spoke, leaning into my anger. "You know that, right? Tell me you know that."

His lips pressed together into a cold, hard line and his eyes blazed. It made my heart race, and I felt a sudden urge to loosen those tight lips with a kiss. *Seriously, Vicky, what is wrong with you?*

"I was perfectly safe," he ground out, keeping himself under control with an effort that left him trembling. "Gessar is dangerous, but I would slay him. The others are of no consequence."

My turn to glare, looking up into Tzaron's fiery gaze. My shoulders shook as I took a step closer and planted my hands on my hips. "So that's what passes for strategic thought in your warband, huh? What does it matter if you kill them? You'll still have sided with a human against the Zrin, and I don't think anyone here will take that well. Gessar's men will try to get their revenge, your horde will tear itself apart. Somewhere in there, you die."

Tail lashing behind him, Tzaron stepped closer. In arm's reach now, I had to crane my neck to look him in the eyes, but neither of us was willing to break eye contact. I swallowed, looking up at the wall of blue-scaled flesh that rose before me. My breath shortened, I squirmed, and a nervous shiver ran down my spine — I'd never been quite so aware of how helpless I was. If he wanted something from me, there'd be nothing I could do to stop him.

And of course that's more exciting than scary. I was such a disappointment to myself, it was almost funny.

"You would live," he whispered after a pause that must have lasted no more than a handful of seconds, though to me it seemed like an eternity. "I made my choice knowing the risks, but they attacked *you* and that is all they need to do to earn a death."

"And wreck all your plans? Your horde would be finished," I shot back. No self-control remained to hold back my snark, and I didn't care if this guy wanted to claim to be the khan of khans or whatever. He'd kill me for my attitude if he wanted to, I was done holding back.

Many possible responses flashed through my mind, but Tzaron surprised me by laughing. That hadn't been on the list, and it only made me angrier.

"You think *I'm* being unreasonable here? Look to yourself, human. If you are right, then perhaps you have saved me — but you have also saved the horde which you fear will conquer your home. How dare you lecture *me* on putting you first when you're doing the same?"

I opened my mouth to respond, but no sound came out. Tzaron looked on, an infuriating grin on his face, as I struggled to find a way out of the contradiction he'd caught me in.

"Fuck you," I explained, lacking a better answer. "I saved your damned *life,* you could at least show me some gratitude, asshole!"

Too much. I didn't even see him move, but my back slammed into the wall, the impact leaving me breathless. Tzaron's rough, powerful hands pinned me against it, his face inches from mine. My heart thumped, my lips were dry, my eyes wide.

"You will not speak to me in that tone," he said, voice heavy and dark, words twining around my mind. I realized I was biting my lip as a tingling sensation ran through my body. Tzaron's fingers tightened on my shoulder, and I said the only thing that popped into my head.

"Yeah? What are you going to do about it if I keep it up?" I licked my lips before continuing. "Asshole."

The rumbling growl that he let out warned me that I was pushing him. I'd swear I saw his heart beating faster, felt his pulse racing. He trembled on the edge of losing control. God knows why, but I had to push it.

"What? We both know you don't have the guts to do anything to me. If you did, you'd have punished me for running away." My voice caught on the word 'punished' and my cheeks warmed. I glared up at him, trying to look fierce and defiant when, inside, I felt anything but confident.

Whether it was the words, the defiant glare, or the skimpy sheet I'd wrapped myself in, something in there was enough to snap the last restraints on Tzaron's behavior. His growl became a snarl of anger and lust and *hunger,* the raw feral power of it making me shudder and gasp, and he ripped the sheet off me in one smooth movement. It tore under his claws, leaving me standing naked in front of him.

Naked, and very aware of the bulge under his kilt. Of his taut, powerful muscles, his claws, his teeth, and tail.

A ragged breath escaped my lips as I struggled with the urge to touch him, to feel his scales under my fingers, his gorgeous six-pack abs under my tongue...

Victoria Ellen Bern, what the hell are you thinking about? my rational brain asked. But that was a tiny voice in the chaotic maelstrom of my mind, my thoughts blowing this way and that like leaves on the storm winds of my emotions.

He was my enemy. I'd promised myself I'd escape from him, that I'd get away and find a way home or die trying. I fixed my thoughts on that, rather that the raw sexual heat that threatened to burn away my misgivings, and brought my hand up fast and hard.

Tzaron was bigger, stronger, better trained. This was a fight I knew I'd lose, which didn't change the fact that it was my only option. My self-defense training was out of date and out of practice, but somehow I hit his wrist and knocked his grip loose. A moment's shock was all the advantage I had, and I made the most of it. Twisting away from the towering Zrin, I darted forward and...

... kissed him full on the lips.

What the actual fuck? This wasn't part of the plan. Apparently, my body had its own plan, though, and Tzaron didn't mind it one bit. His heart pounded, his breath caught, and those powerful arms closed around me. Only I didn't feel trapped by them. I felt safe.

His tongue pressed against my lips, pushing into

my mouth as he lifted me, one hand holding my ass, rough fingers squeezing gently. The other cushioned the back of my neck, holding my head in place for his kiss. With no sign of effort, he lifted me up and held me to him, sending a shiver running through my body.

Pulling at his own clothing, I fumbled with the unfamiliar leather fastenings until he laughed and helped me. Somehow, his clothes came off without him putting me down, and he snagged a fur hanging from the wall with his tail as he carried me into the center of the audience hall.

"This doesn't make us friends," I gasped, coming up for air and realizing just how eager my body was. I'd never been this wet, this desperate to be filled, and one glance at Tzaron's grin told me the bastard knew that.

"Of course not," he agreed too easily, lifting me higher and kissing his way down my neck, my collarbone, down to my breasts. "We are much more than that."

My objection vanished into a shuddering moan as his tongue darted out to tease my nipples. A yelp followed the moan, Tzaron biting down just hard enough to send a shiver of fear and pain and pleasure through my body.

Breathing raggedly, I had no resistance left. Whatever objections I'd harbored were swept away on a tide of lust and need, and I couldn't even remember why I'd wanted to object. I pulled his head to me, gasping and writhing as he chuckled darkly into my breasts, covering them in kisses and licks and bites.

He lowered me to the floor, onto the soft white fur he'd dropped beneath me. Looking down along the length of my body at him, eyes went wide as I saw what was in store for me.

Tzaron's cock was massive, a solid blue length that had to be too big for me. I'd never imagined something that size inside me, and fear of what it might do to me vied for control against my need to find out what it felt like.

Size wasn't the only daunting thing about him. Reaching down, I stroked it and felt the hard texture of scales, utterly unlike any human's cock. And yet it pulsed with a familiar heat, and I bit my lip as Tzaron lifted his lips from my body and drew himself closer.

Scared or not, I didn't hesitate to guide him to me, and Tzaron took the invitation gladly, thrusting hard into my core. Gasping, arching, I spread myself as wide as I could. For the briefest of moments my body resisted the massive, broad, rock-hard cock... but then my muscles relaxed and to my surprised delight Tzaron drove his full length into me. He fit *perfectly,* as though some god had built him for the purpose. The hard scales felt delightfully different from anything else I'd ever felt, and where I'd expected pain, his sudden thrust sent crashing a wave of pleasure roaring through me instead. The force of his thrusts pinned me to the floor, hard and fast and *god* so wonderful.

Neither of us had the patience to take things slowly, not now that the barriers between the two of us were down. I gripped him tight, my legs wrapped around his torso to spur him on, my hands pulling his head down for a kiss. He gave that up easily, kissing my mouth with a rough power that made me squirm.

His chuckle at that only made thing worse, made me want to hide my face as a red glow filled my cheeks. Nipping my neck with needle-sharp teeth, he whispered something I didn't catch in Zrin, and thrust again, even harder, even deeper into my aching pussy that felt fuller than I could have imagined. The ridged, solid surface felt like nothing on Earth as he buried it inside me, withdrew, and thrust again. And again.

We both breathed hard but where Tzaron's breath came and went in a well-controlled cycle, mine devolved into a mix of whimpers and moans and groans. Heart racing, I arched under Tzaron, pushing my body against him and gasped a request. "More. Harder. Please."

He raised his head to meet my gaze, his eyes sparkling with joy and mischief, his grin saying *yes* without words. His next thrust left all control behind, smashing me down to the floor with enough force to let me feel the hard ceramoplastic through the furs. Scrabbling at his back, my nails catching on his scales, I writhed and gasped. Tzaron grabbed my wrists, easily pulling them over my head and pinning them to the floor. One of his hands was enough to grip both my wrists, and now I was truly trapped. My breath caught as I realized how helpless Tzaron had me, and worse, how wonderful that felt. I struggled, tried to pull my arms free, but it was hopeless, and with each move I proved that to myself.

Tzaron's rumbling laugh, dark and powerful, vibrated through me. His cock swelled as I panted and fought, and the combination pushed me over the edge into the wildest orgasm I'd ever had.

Screaming my head off in ecstasy, I shook under him, arching helplessly.

He didn't let up, fucking me hard as I writhed in helpless pleasure under him. My pussy squeezed him tight, and I had just resurfaced from the first orgasm when his dick, that awesome, magnificent alien dick swelled further inside me. I tried to speak, to say something, anything, but words had lost their place in my mind, replaced with a howling storm of pleasure.

All I could do was urge him on, and that wasn't necessary. Tzaron fucked with the strength and endurance of a god, leaving me panting and struggling to gather the ragged bits of my mind together.

My pussy tingled and every thrust stretched me wider, each time a little more, a touch of pain that added spice to the amazing pleasure. I tried to say something, only to find Tzaron's mouth closing over mine, muffling my words and thoughts, his kisses driving me back into a space of pure pleasure.

Even Tzaron had begun to falter, fucking harder and rougher, his breath ragged and heart racing. Tension rose inside him, I saw it in the shiver of his skin, heard it in his snarls, felt it in the tightening of his muscles. That wasn't the only thing tightening —

I bore down on his cock, gripping it inside me, his hardness swelling as I squeezed.

Every thrust set my body aflame with pleasure, the scaled and ridged texture of Tzaron's alien cock stimulating me in ways I'd never dreamed of, sending me tumbling into one orgasm after another, my body shuddering under him until I couldn't take any more. He held himself at the brink, trembling and snarling, fighting the orgasm that was so close.

"Please," I gasped, and he growled at me. The sound nearly drove me into a mind-blowing orgasm, but I held it back. Somehow. "Please. Cum. Cum in me."

I wasn't used to begging, and my brain was too overloaded with sensation to even know which language I used, but Tzaron understood. His lips spread in a hungry, evil grin, and he pounded harder, *harder, **harder**.*

I tried again to move my hands, but his grip never faltered as his cock drove deep inside me. In that moment, I was his in every way that mattered, and somehow that was the hottest thing in the world.

With a final scream of joy, I arched under him and his sharp teeth closed on my shoulder, biting hard enough to break the skin. His cock jerked inside me, his cum flooding me, filling me.

Shuddering, clinging to each other, we both tumbled over the edge into a screaming orgasm that shook the room.

13

TZARON

We lay together on the throne room's floor, Victoria shaking in my arms as I cradled her to me, my body drained as though I'd fought ten battles in a day.

And won each of them, I thought, looking down at the amazing woman whose head rested on my chest. Her breath still ragged, she clung to me like I was a tree-trunk in a flooding river. My arm wrapped around her, cradling her protectively, hand resting on her ass and squeezing gently.

It seemed like neither of us wanted to let go. We were doomed to lie here forever. Twined around each other until we died in this embrace. I chuckled, enjoying the ridiculous image.

"Ahem." Of course, there was always someone to spoil the fun. Careful not to disturb Victoria, I twisted to look at the doorway with my best deadly glare.

"What is it, Zsatia? Why do you interrupt me?"

My glare made seasoned warriors surrender, cowed mutiny in my own ranks, forced an entire town to lay down their weapons and let us in rather than fight. Zsatia didn't pay it even a moment's attention as she folded her arms and leaned against the door frame.

"First, because there are serious matters waiting for your attention, and I don't want your horde to collapse into civil war," she said, voice, face, and ssav devoid of humor. "That would give me far too much work."

I laughed loud enough to make Victoria moan and snuggle into me tighter. Getting control over myself, I shook my head and responded.

"Your concern for me and the members of my horde is noted, Zsatia. Now, what was the second thing?"

"The human is injured, and I cannot speak for her safety if she engages in anything more than light exercise." Her eyes narrowed as she looked around at the chaos we'd left in our wake. "I told you that, and I told *her* that. I didn't think I had to add 'so don't fuck her up and down your throne room till you both pass out' but here we are."

Joy drained from me, replaced by an icy feeling of dread. Lust had gripped me hard enough that I hadn't even considered the risks or Zsatia's warnings. I'd allowed my instincts to take control and risked hurting her. If I'd added to her injuries, I deserved no better than Gessar.

"You told me, and I ignored your warnings," I said as I sat up, cradling my human lover in my arms. She groaned again, squirming a little, but didn't wake. There were no obvious signs of injury aside from my bite marks on her shoulder, but that meant little. I didn't know what to look for on a human, and nor did Zsatia.

"Heal her, Zsatia, and I shall be grateful forever."

Given how much I already owed the medic, it wasn't that persuasive an offer, but I couldn't think of a better one on my way out, heading for Zsatia's healing chambers.

"Of course, sure. Undo all my work and then have me patch it again," Zsatia groused, following me. I didn't need to look to know there was orange in her ssav, humor at my expense. "When you brought her to me, I had to make up half the procedures as I worked. Now you fuck that up and who knows what extra damage you've done this time? But at least your ssav is alive again. That's worth tearing up everything I did for her."

There wasn't much to say to that. She wasn't wrong — our mating had been impulsive, ill-advised, and dangerous. Also, amazing. If I had the choice to make over again, I'd do the same thing, though perhaps not as vigorously. A look down at my ssav was all it took to prove that Victoria was my taru-ma – now that we'd mated, the lines moved and colors shifted once more.

Victoria mumbled something in my arms, squirming and trying to free herself of my grip. I growled down at her.

"Don't be foolish. You are in no state to walk," I said. Instead of taking the hint, she shifted her weight and rolled in my arms to look behind me.

"Did she tell you that? Because I don't think she's operated on a human before, so how would she know?"

Instead of annoying me, Victoria's argument released some of my tension. She was right, we had no way to judge. A sign of serious injury in a Zrin might be normal for a human. My muscles relaxed and I took a deep breath, only then realizing how much I hurt all over. The fight had taken a lot out of me, and I hadn't let myself rest afterward.

If I got a scar from making my taru-ma cum, then I'd carry that scar proudly to my grave.

I didn't put her down, of course. Even if the feebleness of her struggles hadn't warned me that she wasn't ready to support herself, why would I let go of the delightfully squirming female? Holding her was life itself.

The journey to the healing chambers was over all too soon, and once inside I had no excuse to keep her in my arms. With a sigh, I lay her down on one of the strange beds — less strange now that I saw how well a human fit on one.

"I'll have to check her over to see what damage you've done," Zsatia grumbled, pushing between us. Oblivious to the danger pushing herself between us put her in, she began her examination.

Three deep breaths calmed my anger, and I stepped away to let her work. Space was in short supply here, and in my exhaustion I stumbled into the wall. Grabbing blindly for something to restore my balance, I took hold of a recessed handle and pulled.

"Vahtz Enatur ovze Medicha lemurjenze?" the spirit of the room said in its incomprehensible language. Zsatia turned to glare at me as I pushed the handle back into its niche in the wall with an angry snarl.

"Great, now we're all cursed," she said, rolling her eyes. "Whatever that ghost is, it's been quiet for ages."

The booming voice had appeared before, speaking in what I now recognized was a human language. Disturbing any of the switches and buttons ran a risk of enraging it, and we didn't know the right offerings to appease it.

"I take responsibility," I said. "If the room needs to be exorcised, I will arrange it."

"What the actual fuck?" We both turned to look at Victoria, who'd sat up in bed, face pale and blue eyes wide. "The ship still has *power?*"

"There is no danger, Victoria, this ghost has appeared before and it never hurt anyone."

"Ghost?" Victoria snorted and shook her head. "There's no ghost here, idiot. That's the medbay emergency AI."

The last word meant nothing to me, and the

disrespect in the rest made me frown. The human rolled her eyes. "Yes, fine, I know. No one gets away with speaking to you like that. I'll regret saying it. But right now there's something more important than that."

Before I could object that nothing was more important than our relationship, she turned away and pressed her right palm onto an unremarkable part of the wall. Zsatia gasped, and I barely kept my face straight as the wall unfolded, revealing a panel of shiny black stone and a mess of switches.

"That wall... how did we miss that..." Zsatia trailed off as lights glowed on the stone surface. Victoria touched them and they changed color or flowed like water. Her companion spirit materialized at her side, conjuring diagrams of light to help Victoria's sorcery.

"A part of the human magic," I replied, though I wasn't sure myself. But a leader must sound confident, especially when he wasn't. "I brought her for this. She will use this magic better than any Zrin."

As though responding to my words, the floor trembled under our feet and some of the ceiling tiles glowed, illuminating the chamber. The dark shadows in the corners vanished, dispelled by the golden light.

The walls had been white when I first found this place. Now, though, stains covered most of them. Where Zrin made burnt offerings to the Sky Gods for healing, or where the lamps stood, smoke stained the walls in ugly black streaks. Blood marked some of the surfaces, the largest bed had buckled under a weight greater than intended. More of the black stone gleamed under the bright light where it lay set into some of the surfaces, cracked or, in one case, shattered. Wires showed underneath, though I had no clue why. Expensive as wire was to make, the humans had hidden a fortune behind the flat black panel where no one would see.

The harsh light showed Victoria's bruises clearly, and I winced at the sight, my jaw tightening. Every instinct, every fiber of my being, called me to bloody vengeance on those who'd hurt her so.

But she'd forbidden it. She wanted them to live for my sake. Frustration gnawed at my guts like a swarm of k'va beetles were loose in my stomach, and I tried to ignore it by focusing on Victoria's magic. It worked, if only for a little while.

"You should rest," Zsatia said. My tail lashed from side to side at the tone took with my mate, even though I agreed with the sentiment. "You're still my patient, human, and whatever magic you're doing can wait."

Victoria laughed, then winced. "No fucking way. Your medicine is great, but if I can get an autodoc working... there."

Autodoc meant nothing to me, nor to Zsatia. We both turned at a hissing sound to find a human-sized sarcophagus opening, white fog leaking from it. Victoria joined us looking at it.

"What is this 'autodoc'?" I asked, in awe of my human's sudden magic.

"An *auto*matic *doc*tor," she said, enunciating carefully to make sure we followed, then translating the human words into Sky Tongue.

I hung on every word, not for the information she gave us — though that knowledge might prove vital later — but for the beautiful, song-like sound of her voice would have held me enraptured if she started reciting the names of her ancestors.

"On its own, it can only handle simple injuries," she continued. "Someone needs to tell it what it's supposed to do, but from that point it can handle almost any injury."

"Any injuries, or any *human* injuries?" Zsatia asked. A good question, and one I'd never have thought to ask.

Victoria opened her mouth, closed it, gathered her brows together. "I don't know. These things aren't top of the line, and humans designed them to be used on humans. The basics are probably the same, though, so it should treat a broken bone in anyone with a skeleton?"

Her worried tone dampened my excitement, though this was still a joyous discovery. A magic coffin that healed injured warriors would be a powerful tool, but someone would have to use it before we could count on it. Still, that didn't matter as much as having something that would heal *her*.

"We can discuss the limits later," I said, stepping forward and sweeping Victoria off her feet. She clung to me without hesitation, and the warmth of her skin sent a wave of joy through me. "First, you must recover."

I lowered her into the sarcophagus, a cold mist floating around us, making my skin tingle. It took an effort to let go of her and step back, letting the off-white cover close over her. Surrendering my taru-ma to this magic box was difficult, but I had to trust that she knew what she was doing.

"Cheer up," Zsatia said, clapping me on the shoulder. "You caught her to show you human magic

— if this messes up then you know not to trust any of their blessings."

Which wasn't the point at all but still accurate. I bit back a snarl and stalked from her chamber, looking for work to bury myself in while my beloved healed.

14

VICTORIA

*A*utodocs are weird. The fog of nanoparticles, cold and stinging, settled into my skin, numbing it. A deep breath flooded my lungs with it, and my worries melted away. As did my sense of time, and my anxiety, and most of my thoughts.

I'd heard of people locking themselves inside an autodoc and just letting everything slip away — a race to see if they'd starve before the autodoc's supplies ran low and it ejected its passenger. True or myth, I saw the point of the stories now. This blissful sensation, like being carried in clouds of drugs, was better than what waited for me outside.

A nagging feeling reminded me that Tzaron

wasn't in here with me. He needed to stay or lose control of his horde.

The truth washed over me like a cold rain, washing away the warm happiness. If he couldn't be here, I'd have to go out there to be with him. As though that thought was a trigger, the autodoc opened, blinding light shining through the healing fog. I sat up, rubbed my eyes, and took a deep breath. Mind clearing, I kept my eyes shut and sorted through my memories, trying to put them all into context.

"No further," a soft Zrin voice said, and a sharp edge tapped my throat. "We have a matter to settle, you and I."

My muscles froze, my heart turned to lead, and adrenaline cleared the fog from my brain. The Zrin had threatened me before and it hadn't ended well for anyone. Was this revenge for that? Cautiously opening my eyes, I saw a tall, lean Zrin woman, knife held at my throat in a steady hand, torso wrapped in bandages and blood seeping through. Something familiar about the face gave me pause, and I remembered the Zrin warrior I'd shot back at the Vale. It seemed a hundred years ago, but I doubted I'd ever forget the face of the first person I'd shot.

And now she looked at me, eyes blazing and muscles taut, ready to take her vengeance. Crap.

Tearing my gaze from her, I looked around the room. Zsatia stood against the furthest wall, motionless aside from a writhing ssav full of red and white tendrils. It took me a moment to see why she looked so frightened, because the two Zrin flanking her blended into the medbay so well that my gaze slid over them. Their knives didn't, though, giving them away where the tips dug into Zsatia's scales. Once I'd spotted the blades, following them up to the hand, then to the torso, was easy.

Well, that's not good, I told myself, looking back at the one who threatened me. Her skin didn't blend with the environment. Instead it was a sickly blue, paler than most Zrin, paler than I remembered her from the attack. *Okay, maybe I didn't kill her, but I hurt her.*

It wasn't much comfort when she had a knife to my throat.

"What do you want?"

"Your head on a stick," the injured Zrin shot back. "A pity I have to give up that pleasure if I'm to live."

She pressed her knife into my skin and I stayed

as still as I could. One sudden motion would open my neck from ear to ear, and even if I fell straight back into the autodoc, I didn't know if it would keep me alive long enough to fix the damage.

Perhaps my attacker realized I wouldn't be able to speak like this, or perhaps her arm tired. She lowered the blade and grabbed my arm, fingers gripping hard enough to bruise, and dragged me out of the autodoc. Either she was too weak to support me, or she didn't care to try, and I tumbled naked to the hard floor. Stripped of the nanoparticles' protection, the cold ceramoplastic chilled me to the bone. But that was the only discomfort I felt — the autodoc had healed everything else, cracked ribs and bruises and everything. Despite the menace of the Zrin attacker looming over me, I grinned as I rolled to my feet. Even the ache in my muscles was gone, fixed by that marvelous machine.

The Zrin snarled at me but made no move to follow. "It looks like the magic tomb has repaired you. My turn."

"I told you, Heshra," Zsatia said, voice a hiss of anger. "It won't work on Zrin. This is a fool's errand."

Still looking at me, Heshra bared her teeth and beckoned with the tip of her knife. I weighed my options. Run for the door? Even injured, Heshra would catch me before I'd gone two steps. Fight? It was, at best, three on two. Not good odds given that I didn't know how to fight. That left compliance and waiting for an opportunity to get away.

"If this magic won't heal me, why bother keeping you alive? This wound will kill me before long." Heshra glared at me, eyes narrow and lit with a spark of fury. Mouth suddenly dry, I swallowed and nodded.

"It might heal you, it might not," I said, hating the way my voice shook. It was like being locked in a cage with a tiger, and any move I made could be my last. "There's nothing to lose trying, though. Get in and I'll see if I can get it to work."

Heshra hissed something unintelligible at me before hauling herself into the sarcophagus with an effort that made me wince. I'd intended to kill her when I shot her, yes, but seeing her injured hadn't been part of the deal.

If she'd been well enough, she'd have joined the Zrin kicking me to death, I told myself. *She doesn't deserve my sympathy.*

It sounded simple, but I couldn't quite bring myself to believe it. Of all the Zrin, Heshra was the one with a reason to want me dead. That put her a step above the assholes who'd attacked me, and since I'd saved them from Tzaron's vengeance, it wouldn't be fair to let her die.

"Pity I'm not qualified to use this thing," I muttered under my breath in English. Heshra looked at me suspiciously.

"Lie down and breathe deep," I told her. "The fog has... healing magic?"

I wanted to give a better explanation, but I didn't understand the technology well enough myself. Explaining in English would be hard enough, but in Eskel? Not a chance — magic it would have to be.

Heshra's eyes narrowed, but she followed my instructions, lying back uncomfortably in the too-small space. After a couple of breaths, though, she stopped squirming and relaxed as I closed the lid over her.

"She dies, you die," one of her nearly invisible followers hissed. "Both of you."

"Idiot," Zsatia replied with such withering contempt that I half expected the other Zrin to fall over dead from sheer embarrassment. "Threatening a doctor never improves things for the patient. Besides, how long do you think you'll live once you murder us?"

"You'll still be dead," the warrior blustered, gray and amber patterns appearing on his camouflaged skin, letting me focus on him properly. Buoyed by Zsatia's disrespect for them, I added my voice to hers.

"Yes, *we know,* you didn't have to tell us," I said. My voice no longer shook, and some tension left my limbs. "You big strapping dangerous warriors will carve up two peaceful females if I don't get this to work. Now, are you going to shut up and let me focus, or are you trying to get your leader killed?"

I turned away before he managed a response, uncovering a control panel and trying to make sense of it. There was one advantage to it being a human model, I could read everything without Catula having to translate it. That might make up for the human design — other species had far superior technology, but what use would that be if I couldn't read the instructions?

The diagnostic screen showed error after error. Brain scans were all over the place, indicating half a dozen forms of nerve damage, several of them mutually exclusive. I pressed the 'Ignore' button and moved on.

Circulatory system? Heshra, the autodoc reported, had overdosed on multiple drugs I'd never heard of, and her blood pressure was dangerously low. Her blood type was 'unclassified' and no transfusion material was available. Not good news, but what could I do? *Ignore.*

Her skin, according to the display, was badly burned, scarred, and infected with an exciting variety of deadly fungi.

It didn't even have a wrong guess for what had happened to Heshra's skeleton. Doing the computer equivalent of throwing its hands up in the air, the autodoc simply labeled that whole tab *ERROR* and refused to speculate.

Respiration surprised me with a passing score. Zrin and human breathing patterns seemed to be close enough to one another that the autodoc proclaimed Heshra healthy in that regard.

"Okay, you bucket of bolts. How do I fix a wound?" Talking to it wouldn't help, so I set to working my way through the menus and sub-menus, cursing the computer's lack of user-friendliness. It was, admittedly, not designed to be used by a random member of the public — the only people who ought to be using these controls were doctors and qualified maintenance personnel. I was neither.

Catula did his best too, interfacing with the

autodoc directly. Now, if only I'd thought to load him down with a medical program, he might have managed something, but no such luck. I'd left that to the Vale's doctors instead.

The only thing to say for his help was that together we figured out what we couldn't do quicker than I would have on my own. We couldn't hope to get a general treatment for a Zrin set up, but in Heshra we had a patient with a known injury. No need to rely on diagnostics that didn't recognize a Zrin.

We'd just have to guide the damned thing ourselves, and that was a task that Catula was well suited to. His skill with computer interfaces let me get around the several layers of security designed to stop unauthorized personnel from doing exactly this and soon we were able to start tagging Heshra's wounds. Starting deep inside her injury and working outward, we marked every injury we could find for repair, hoping that techniques used on humans would work on Zrin, too.

It was stressful work, and risky. If we left any bleeding inside her, she'd die of it and no doubt her followers would blame me and Zsatia. But there were only so many times I could double-check the internal sutures, and it wasn't as though I knew what kind of problem to look for.

Persuading the autodoc to repair Heshra's skin turned out to be a tougher challenge. The computer didn't recognize the material as skin, and having felt Tzaron's, I couldn't blame it. The rough texture of his scales, the smooth way they moved with his muscles, the electric feeling as I ran my hands over his... *focus, Vicky, focus.* Ahem. My point was that his skin was nothing like a human's.

"Manual control it is then," I muttered, taking over and doing my best with the unfamiliar controls. After far too long, I had to admit I'd done everything I could and stepped back from the sarcophagus.

"Well?" One of Heshra's guards snapped the question at me, and it took an effort not to snap back.

"She'll be okay. She just needs to rest in the autodoc for a while." *I hope.* Keeping my voice calm was an effort. Today was already too much. "I've stopped the bleeding and closed the wound — so *now* will you let Zsatia go?"

A tense moment passed and then the invisible Zrin relaxed, their camouflage fading back to normal ssavs. Keeping my relief from showing wasn't easy, though Zsatia remained infuriatingly calm as she stepped away from her erstwhile captors.

"*Now* may I get back to work? There are other injured warriors to see to." The acid in Zsatia's voice could have melted through the hull, and I enjoyed the resultant squirming from the guards. They weren't completely without conscience, it seemed.

One nodded. "But you both stay here, where we can watch you. If you have tricked us and Heshra dies in your machine, we will avenge her."

I sighed. In their place I'd have done the same, but then I wouldn't have started this stupid plan. What was I going to do for the hours the autodoc needed?

IF YOU GUESSED 'SLEEP' then you're right, I should have gotten some. the autodoc's treatment left me too wired to consider a nap. Instead, I searched around the medbay, trying to dig out anything that still worked.

A lot of it didn't, which didn't surprise me in the slightest. The impact with the cliff must have been terrible, and the shocking thing was that *anything* still worked. But the colony pods were hardy things, designed to take a beating, and more had survived the crash than I'd expected. I should have known as soon as I woke up — I'd seen the angle the pod lay at. The floor should be at a thirty-degree angle or more, so the fact that we were standing straight gave away the fact that the gravity generators still functioned.

The damage was still bad, but some things were salvageable. Two of the beds still had working diagnostic suites and getting those back online only took a few minutes. The medicine maker was more of a challenge, full of error codes and demands for a qualified technician. Understandable, one look inside it showed a delicate network of tubes and wires, several of them snapped.

Catula had the construction diagrams in his datastore, which let me fix the most important parts. Getting them to work with Zrin physiology wouldn't be as easy, but hopefully Zsatia would get some use out of them. She'd need supplies to take advantage of the diagnostic data or to reload the maker, so my next task was unlocking the supply room. A frustrating challenge, and impossible without Count Catula: he provided evidence that I had a colony level clearance from Vale.

It still took ages of arguing to convince it to open

the door for me without explicit approval from the local leadership. Time in which the Zrin stared at me like a crazy lady. My cheeks burned as I tried to ignore them, knowing how it looked — here was the crazy alien, arguing with a section of wall. At least Catula was on my side, glaring at the door and reinforcing my arguments over the local network.

At last the door slid open, lights flickering on in the chamber beyond and illuminating pure horror. A fleshy mass slid toward me, a monster from the holo-shows I never watched, and I recoiled, terrified of this new monstrosity.

My fear put my reaction a moment ahead of the Zrin, but where I screamed and fell over my feet, they responded more practically. Their knives sank into the *thing* before I'd finished screaming, and the avalanche of flesh rolled to a stop just shy of my feet. I caught my breath, staring at it.

"What in the Skyless Depths is that thing?" one of the guards whispered, voice shaking. In comparison, his comrade sounded delighted.

"Yes, human, what monster have we slain? We are heroes now, felling a demon."

Cautiously, I reached out to prod the awful thing. It felt like a dead body, a dead *human* body. I knew that feeling all too well after the Crash, when every survivor took part in the burial of those we'd lost. Cold, dead, no sign of residual warmth... this thing was long dead.

Or had never lived. A hysterical laugh broke out of my throat and I forced it down with difficulty when the Zrin stared at me.

"Not a monster," I gasped. "Not anything, really. This is sprayskin, artificial human skin. Some canisters in there must have ruptured in the Crash and, well, it expands so..."

I trailed off, looking into the storage chamber and cursing. The artificial flesh filled it, burying any usable supplies. If anything useful remained under that mess, it would take careful excavation to find it. Careful, *disgusting* excavation, digging through a material that mimicked human flesh all too well.

That's a job for someone else, I decided, scooting away from the horrible mass and pulling myself to my feet. The Zrin guards cautiously moved in to pluck their knives from the boneless mass.

"Your people make horrible wonders," one said, and I wondered whether that was a compliment or a criticism. A bit of both, perhaps? Both guards backed off from the 'monster' and by some strange collective decision, we all took a seat. Repairs on the medbay were officially on hold, and instead we took to swapping stories to pass the time. It was good practice for my Eskel, and they had fascinating stories to share. So did I, it turned out. Vale Settlement's arrival on Crashland fascinated and amused in equal measure, and after a few tales I wondered if I might make some friends.

15

TZARON

"*S*ire, what are you doing?" Krosak's insistent whine hurt my ears like claws on slate and I struggled to keep my temper. "Sparing Gessar is a mistake."

Privately, I agreed with him. Perhaps humans were different, perhaps my human taru-ma was an idealist or merely naïve, but amongst the Zrin, leaving such a beast alive was asking for another attempted overthrow. Still, the decision was made — to go back on it now would just make things worse.

And Victoria had a point. Killing Gessar and his lackeys would risk the horde coming apart like an over-ripe jyll fruit left in the sun.

"Gessar knows he's lost this round," I replied,

hoping to finish this conversation quickly. We stood in the great hall, waiting for the supplicants I'd put off in favor of a swift trial. Listening to the weaker members of the horde had proved a valuable tool in my rise to power, and I did not want to keep my people waiting. "It may sting, but he knows he owes Victoria-ma his life. No doubt he'll talk himself out of honoring that debt, but for the time being we're safe."

Krosak made an unconvinced noise but didn't press any further. I clapped him on the shoulder. "Cheer up, my friend. We've made a conquest no other Zrin has. With my mate to repair the palace, soon we shall be an unstoppable force and sweep the world."

My lieutenant looked slightly ill at the prospect of that much war, but still he nodded enthusiastically. I knew him well enough to know his reasoning: as long as we were winning, his position was secure, and with that so was his life. He'd built a clan of opportunists and held their loyalty only so long as they prospered.

Taking my seat, I let Krosak usher in the first petitioners, which he did with a flourish. First came a woman, here to complain about her neighbor stealing her supply of salt. Behind her, in a line that stretched out of the palace, were others, all with equally important claims that could only be settled by their leader.

Of all the lesser warleaders that followed me, only Krosak understood why I listened to these petty problems. All the others were delighted to have these headaches dropped on my shoulders. I had no complaints, for two reasons. First, I liked helping those who followed me, and second, it gave me the chance to make a tangible improvement in their lives. Heshra, Gessar, and the rest might control their warriors, but making these judgments gave me a hold on the rest of their followers.

But only if I did a good job of it. Settling down for a long day's work, I tried to keep my mind on mysterious salt disappearances and off the thought of Victoria's beautiful, sexy body. It would be a hard-fought battle.

I HEARD the voices as I approached the medical chamber, and the sound of Victoria's put a spring in my step until I heard who she was talking to. A Zrin male answered her words and I burst into the room, ready to protect my love from this interloper.

Only to stop in surprise at the sight that waited for me. Two Zrin patients waited there, one in conversation with Victoria, the other working alongside Zsatia at one of the counters. No weapons out, no fresh injuries on any of them — my mate was safe, or as safe as could be hoped. My gaze flicked over her to check her wounds, then again, slower, to appreciate what I saw. The last time I'd seen her, bruises and cuts covered her skin. All had vanished, healed by the human magic of the box behind me. A crushing pressure I'd refused to acknowledge lifted from my heart — no lasting harm done, then.

The room itself hadn't been so lucky. A hidden door lay open, blocked by some gelatinous monstrosity. Dead or unconscious, it lay unmoving on the threshold like a monster in a story after the hero has passed by.

And yet the others ignored it. Zsatia and her companion worked with their backs to the new doorway, and Victoria spoke with the other Zrin, practicing her grasp of Sky Tongue. I suppressed a murderous upwelling of jealousy, forcing even breaths — I knew that Victoria would not betray me, she was my fated mate, but *I* should be the one teaching her, speaking with her, spending time on her.

"Skyless Depths, what happened here?" I demanded. My mind kicked over the possibilities, but nothing rational came to mind. Both Zrin warriors jumped up and saluted, their ssavs perfect displays of respect. *Too* perfect, giving them away as Heshra's scouts — no other Zrin would be able to control their emotional displays so precisely, and I wondered what they were hiding.

Zsatia laughed, a cold sarcastic laugh that did nothing to lessen the tension. "Nothing much. Just the attack of the living ooze, a hostage negotiation, and the ongoing experiment into whether the human magic works on Zrin injuries."

One of the scouts hissed at her, hand twitching towards the hilt of his knife, then away. My muscles tensed at that, looking around carefully. Heshra's troops were sneaky, and whatever was happening here I didn't want to discover that there were more of them hidden against the walls.

No one. Either there were no more of them, or their reinforcements were too skilled for me to spot.

Zsatia laughed again, waving a hand at the warrior who, despite the control he had over his ssav, looked increasingly unhappy.

"Do you think that I'm afraid of you *now?*" she

asked. "Under Lord Tzaron's eyes? These two are here to force us to work wonders.

"Are you well, taru-ma?" I said to Victoria in Sky Tongue. She nodded carefully.

"We had a little trouble earlier, but we're all friends now," she said. "Isn't that right, Jokzar?

Jokzar smiled and shrugged, too casually for it to be genuine, and I flexed my fingers. Claws slid out, and now I had everyone's attention.

"What happened?" My question came out a growl, despite my best efforts to keep myself calm. I'd already pardoned those who'd attacked my mate once. If this pair had hurt her, threatened her, done anything to harm her, I'd tear them apart.

Victoria glanced around nervously, from the scouts to my claws to Zsatia, but she was spared the need to answer me by a hissing sound at my back.

I spun to see the sarcophagus opening, a fine white mist escaping. A brittle silence fell over the room, all of us staring at the autodoc. No one moved, no one breathed, until a Zrin hand emerged from the whiteness and grabbed the sarcophagus's rim.

Heshra pulled herself into view, her pupils wide and body shaking. Stretching, twisting, she moved with a fluid grace I'd thought lost to her injury. I would have given her a perhaps three in ten chance of surviving her injury, and no chance of walking without pain. Yet here she was, vaulting out of the autodoc and proving that human magic was incredible.

"It worked," Heshra cried, shaking her fists to the Sky in triumph. "I'm alive, I'm whole, I — what are you all looking at?"

Her eyes narrowed and the joy left her. No one spoke, all of us looking at her wound, or rather where her wound had been. Following our gazes, she looked down and her ssav erupted in a confusion of colors. All save the part over her injury, which stayed a pale pinkish color not far from the hue of my Victoria's skin.

Heshra stared at the discolored patch for a heartbeat before snapping her eyes up to focus on Victoria. "What have you *done,* human?"

Victoria wasn't stupid. She stepped to my side swiftly, letting me shield her from harm. Surely Heshra wasn't so angry that she'd pick a fight with me? It would doom her and her warband, no matter who won.

"I didn't, I mean, it's an accident," Victoria said, stumbling over her words. "I didn't know the autodoc would use sprayskin, I swear."

Heshra took another step, putting her in striking

distance of my mate, so I moved into her path. "Have care, that is my taru-ma you threaten."

For a moment, I thought she would strike me. I almost hoped for it — let me settle a threat to my beloved with violence and I'd feel better about letting the others go. But at the last moment she saw sense and withdrew to a safe distance.

"Whoever she is to you, she has scarred me. Damaged my ssav. Tried to kill me. Sire, I demand my vengeance."

Zsatia saved me from having to answer, which was for the best. "Vengeance? Heshra, are you mad or just an idiot? The human saved your life. You attacked her people, she defended herself from you, and then healed you from a wound that should have been lethal. Now you're so upset over a scar that you want her dead? If she wanted to harm you, she'd have killed you."

The withering glare she shot Heshra as she spoke ought to have put Heshra back in the autodoc. The scout leader's ssav shifted and twisted, angry red mixing with the gray of shame. Finally, she nodded and looked past me to Victoria.

"Zsatia is right," she said, begrudging every word. "I apologize for threatening you. Your debt is cleared."

With that, she wheeled around and marched to the exit, her followers scrambling to keep up and give her back her clothes. She vanished into the palace, still dressing as she went, and I turned back to my mate, waiting to hear what had happened here.

16

VICTORIA

*A*fter that excitement, things settled down into a curious equilibrium. I got on with the work of repairing whatever I could. I'd never been a skilled mechanic, but I managed the basics and fortunately that was all I needed. Most of the systems damaged in the crash were either easy fixes or destroyed outright, with little in between.

The datastore helped a lot. In Vassily's scramble to fill it, he'd included full maintenance manuals for everything the colony pods carried on our flight. Between them and Count Catula's assistance, my skill grew and with it, my confidence. It helped that I was used to picking up skills as I went, another legacy of my time as a teacher in an underfunded district. I'd lost count of the times I'd found myself half an hour ahead of the class on the topic they were learning.

Vassily would have said to work slowly, I know. Then the Zrin wouldn't know how fast I *could* work, and I could get away with slacking off. I grinned at the thought, figuring if Vassily wouldn't approve I must be doing something right. And besides, the harder I worked, the more of the palace I got to see.

It was strange, like a dark reflection of Vale's mega-pod. Only a small part was in use, the rest behind doorways labeled with blood-red warnings. I might not read the Zrin script, but even I understood the gist of the messages: *Danger of Death, No Entry, Yes That Means You.*

Those weren't the only areas that were off limits to me. Several of the warbands had homes inside the pod, marked by painted boundaries, and I made a note of who nested where. You never knew what might come in handy, and there were some Zrin I wanted to avoid.

To my surprise, though, Gessar's Zrin turned out to be less of a menace than I'd feared. At first, I'd tensed when I saw them, made sure I had a heavy tool at hand just in case. But they kept a respectful distance and never bothered me. After a couple of days of that, I relaxed. Perhaps Gessar had enough honor to appreciate me sparing him.

A week passed without incident, days spent working hard, evenings with Tzaron when he was free of the burdens of leadership. Each night he wanted to know what I'd fixed, even if it took an hour for me to explain the basic principles of what I'd done.

But, whether or not he understood it, he always appreciated my work. That was more than my fellow humans had done.

"Tzaron," I asked one evening after a particularly frustrating time trying to explain why the data cabling mattered. "What are those forbidden areas? You've sealed off most of the pod, and there are a lot of things I can't fix without going in there."

A little bend in the truth. I still had plenty of work to do without crossing those borders, but dammit, I wanted to know.

Tzaron gave me an odd look, surprisingly intense, and thought about it before answering my question with a question of his own. "Why do you work so hard for us? For me? We have raided and looted your home, injured and perhaps killed your followers. Taken you prisoner, and you nearly died at our hands. Yet you cooperate. Why?"

My turn to pause, turning that over and over in my mind. In the end, I decided that the truth would work better than any lie I could come up with. "Because the horse might learn to sing."

Tzaron frowned, and I shook my head. "Sorry, an old Earth joke. There was a teacher, long ago, who offended a king. Sentenced to die, he told the king that, in exchange for his life, he would teach the king's favorite horse to sing. The king, intrigued, gave him one year to prove his claim."

Tzaron looked confused, so I added, "A horse is an animal to be ridden."

"Ah, like a drogara," he said, face clearing. Remembering the sight of those white-furred monsters bearing down on me, I shuddered, but it was close enough.

"So the teacher sang to the horse — the *drogara,* day after day. Tended it, fed it, cared for it. And when his students came to deliver food, they asked why he would do something so ridiculous with such commitment.

"'Ah,' he said to them, 'In a year, many things may change. The king might pardon me, or, if he dies, his heir may pardon all prisoners as is the custom. Or I may see a way to escape and vanish into the hills. Or, if none of those things happen, perhaps the damned drogara can learn to sing.'"

Tzaron blinked and then laughed. "That is a fine story and an excellent lesson."

"Not the one you think, Tzaron," I said. "There's the lesson about patiently waiting for a chance to escape, yes. But also, the work I'm doing isn't useful to you. Not in the long run. I can make things some work, for a while. Then they'll fail in new ways that I can't fix. A singing drogara might be an amazing sight, but what actual good is it?"

Tzaron nodded, and to my surprise, he smiled. "Ah, very good. You may as well gain credit for doing the work as well as you can, when it won't help your captors. But, useful as fixing these magics is, it's not why I brought you here."

"Yeah, my 'magic' of leadership." It wasn't easy to say that without laughing.

"That, and another thing I haven't yet showed you. Taru-ma, you asked about the forbidden areas. Come with me and I shall show you what I keep hidden there."

METAL CREAKED under us as Tzaron led me deeper into the pod's twisted halls. As soon as we passed the warning markers, dark shadows swallowed us, and Tzaron vanished into the blackness. Swallowing nervously, I followed. Ahead of us, an eerie cry rang out, strange and unsettling, like nothing a human or a Zrin throat would produce.

I don't believe in ghosts, I told myself firmly, only for some mischievous part of my mind to answer, *but do they believe in us?*

I hadn't gone two steps before Tzaron wrapped his tail around my wrist. The unexpected touch made me jump, and I only just resisted the urge to scream.

"Follow carefully, the route is perilous," he warned, drawing me further into the darkness. Gentle tugs from his tail guided me first to one side, then the other, around invisible obstacles. It didn't take long for me to work out where he was taking me. This corridor would bring us to the observation deck at the very top of the pod. Designed to give a sweeping view of the surrounding colony, I wondered what I'd see from this one.

We walked in the dark for what felt like hours before I saw light leaking from a doorway ahead. Not the steady light of the sun or an electric light, it flickered like a flame on the verge of going out. It still illuminated enough of the hall to show me what Tzaron had guided me around. The stress of the crash had buckled the decking, tearing it into razor-sharp flaps gleaming in the reddish light. I swallowed, hands trembling, and glanced over my shoulder into the inky black. How close had I come to slicing myself open back there? This maze of deadly metal edges and falls to the level below made for a good defensive barrier, especially if no one knew there was anything of value at the far end.

I forgot about the deathtrap we'd walked through as Tzaron guided me into the observation deck. Above us, the great dome had cracked, and I realized the eerie howls had just been the wind whistling through the gaps. Above the dome hung the night sky, stars twinkling in alien constellations I still wasn't used to.

Under the dome, everything was a mess. Benches and tables had tumbled everywhere in the impact, sections of wall had popped open, and the decking had buckled here too. One table had been righted and re-purposed as a kind of altar. And on that altar sat the source of the light. A jet-black cube, perhaps a foot to a side, sat there, patterns of flames visible through its sides.

I blinked at it, stunned. The fires formed letters, scrolling as I watched. This was technology far beyond the Zrin, and it didn't look like anything human or Prytheen.

"This is our god-cube," Tzaron said, answering before I asked the question. "Every nation of the Zrin holds one. It is almost what defines a nation. The Sky Gods left them to test us, there are many puzzles in each, and solving even one brings great prestige."

"Why do you have it hidden away here, then? Shouldn't you be showing it off to everyone?" I edged closer to the cube as I spoke, peering into the dark stone and trying to make out the script. Nothing I recognized, which was disappointing but not surprising — I only knew a handful of human alphabets, let alone any alien ones.

"Because many will say it isn't mine," Tzaron said, stepping close behind. "I took it from the Far Hills tribe in a raid. Display it openly and someone will try to take it from me."

"Keep it hidden and it does you no good. You need to make it unequivocally *yours*."

"Ah, you understand my problem," Tzaron said, nodding and putting a hand on my shoulder. "My first plan was to solve a puzzle or two, to show I have the blessing of the Sky Gods. But they are impenetrable to me."

I leaned into him, feeling his solid muscles move as he slid his free hand over the cube, flicking through puzzle after puzzle. They meant nothing to me, strange diagrams and incomprehensible text blurring together, and I shook my head.

"You brought me here to help solve this? I can't even read the language."

"You can, you *will,* manage." Tzaron said with total confidence that made me shiver. I didn't want to disappoint him, which was an odd thing to feel for my kidnapper.

Come on, Vicky, is it any weirder than wanting to fuck him? My brain had a point, I admitted reluctantly.

"Fine, I'll do my best, but on my own that won't be much."

"You won't be on your own. Here, take these."

From a pouch at his waist he retrieved the datastore, passing them across to me. I snatched them up before he could change his mind, tapping the wristband and feeling a rush of relief as Count Catula appeared perched on a nearby table. He preened, washing himself as though nothing strange was going on.

"Okay, fine. With that, I can at least try," I said, thinking about it. Catula had the Eskel script in his memory stores, or at least what the Vale had available. The datastore might have any useful information imaginable in it — or nothing of value at all. Vassily had just filled it with whatever he could lay his hands on. I turned it over and over in my hands, weighing it and the future, and deciding to take a risk. "Why should I solve the puzzles, though? This isn't like the repair work upstairs. It's not teaching a drogara to sing, solving this will give you a lot more power. How does that help *me?*"

The looks that flickered across Tzaron's face would have been funny if I hadn't been so nervous. Confusion gave way to anger, to annoyance, to confusion again. This wasn't a man used to hearing someone say no, and I didn't blame the people around him for that. I almost gave in the moment anger flickered in his eyes, and his followers didn't have the same margin of safety around him that I did.

I held my tongue, matching his gaze and forcing myself not to cave until he responded.

"You will help my horde," he started, and I cut him off.

"Nope. Not interested. Your horde invaded my

home and kidnapped me, I don't have any reason to help them."

I admit it, I enjoyed the little flash of anger in his gaze at that. My heart sped up and I chewed on my lip as the feeling of danger swept through me, leaving a familiar tingle behind.

"Do it because I tell you to," he tried.

"And what will you do if I won't? You can't hurt me, not when you need my brain working for you. If you threaten to go after my friends, well, that's exactly why I don't want to strengthen your horde."

"Do it because..." this time Tzaron's words trailed off into silence and he looked down at me, eyes blazing. Somehow I found the strength to meet his gaze and he was the one who looked away, throwing his hands in the air with a snarl. "I give up, human. What is it you want?"

There was something intoxicating about this minor victory, getting him to ask me rather than order me to fix his problem. My cheeks heated and I smiled, trying to keep calm.

"I want the same thing you do, Tzaron. I want answers."

He looked back at me and frowned, eyes narrowing. "Is that all?"

"You haven't heard the questions yet."

That got a laugh out of him, a low rumble that made me quiver, and he sank down into a crouch, back against a wall covered in advertising. A hologram of the rising sun framed my alien captor like a halo, and I caught my breath. Few men managed to look both powerful *and* beautiful, but Tzaron was a work of art. I could have stared at him for hours, paying attention to the details of his form, the way his scales fit together and the way they changed color as his ssav reflected his emotional state. Muscles in his chest moving with each breath, his long and dexterous fingers flexing slightly, just enough for me to wonder what they'd feel like on my skin.

Even his arrogant smile was more sexy than annoying. *I know what you're thinking,* it said. *I know what you want.* And that made me blush brighter, but I did my best to focus on our deal and not on the bulge growing under the folds of his kilt.

"Where are the colonists?" I asked, blurting out the first question in my mind that *wasn't* about Tzaron. "There should be a thousand or more humans here. What did you do with them?"

"Do? Nothing."

"Then where are they?"

Tzaron frowned, and I swallowed, waiting for an

unpleasant answer. Killed by Zrin, eaten by wildlife, starved before they figured out what to eat — there were a thousand ways to die on Crashland, but *some* sign should have remained of them.

"I saw no humans here when I found this place. It was only nine days after the Night of Falling Stars, and I did not know what a human was, but I saw no one leaving, nor any trail."

I'd never imagined what the Crash must have looked like to the native Zrin, and I shivered at the thought now. A sudden rain of meteors battering their world, starting fires and upsetting the wildlife all over the planet — and Tzaron went *toward* the largest impact. Stupid, brave, or crazy?

A bit of all three, probably.

"They must have gone somewhere," I said. I believed Tzaron, but he had to have some idea of what happened to the colonists.

He shook his head. "I suppose they must, but wherever it is, they went there quickly and left no tracks. You would know better than I, but to me it looked like no one had looted the place when I arrived.

That made me frown. I hadn't questioned it before, but thinking back, it didn't look like anything had been taken. Tools, medical supplies, comms equipment — everything was where it had fallen in the crash.

"Was the hatch open when you arrived?"

"Yes," Tzaron answered, getting a faraway look in his eyes. "The valley still burned, so we couldn't reach it for days, but it was open. We kept watch from above the valley and saw nothing move. Once the fire burned out and the ramp cooled, I went inside and explored. No one was there, no sign of anyone either. It was as though the Sky Gods had thrown this down to me as a sign of my right to rule. A palace from the sky, a wondrous seat for my empire."

"An empire you haven't conquered yet." I couldn't resist the jibe, and Tzaron tried to glare at me. It would have been more intimidating if he'd been able to keep the smile off his face.

"If I worried about little details like that, I'd never achieve anything."

His casual hand wave made the joke obvious, but there was a harder truth behind it. His dreams were ambitious, though that might be a polite way to say insane. Welding this disparate mob of killers and bandits into a working society? It sounded impossible, but I'd read enough history to know better. Sometimes people only achieved power because of their unshakable belief that they would win.

And if anyone could do it, Tzaron could. Which brought me back on topic.

"If the colonists didn't go anywhere, and they aren't buried in a mass grave, there's only one possibility left," I said, thinking my logic through as I spoke. My conclusion was inescapable. "They're *still here.*"

Tzaron frowned, opened his mouth to object, snapped it shut again. "My palace is big, perhaps big enough to hide a few humans if they stayed in the forbidden areas. But a thousand? Impossible."

"Oh, they're in the forbidden areas." Excitement getting the better of me, I grabbed Tzaron's hand and squeezed. "They're still in stasis. The crash must have damaged the timers, and they're stuck down in the hold."

Something lit up in Tzaron's eyes. Or perhaps it was my own excitement reflected back at me? He squeezed back, sending a wave of desire up my arm and stopping my breath for a moment. My cheeks heated and I was reduced to stammering.

"The lower forbidden areas are deathtraps, unexplored," he said, taking advantage of my loss of composure to interrupt my speech. "No light at all, and the damage is worse there than up here. What little we've seen of them meant nothing to us, though I suspect you would understand them. No matter. You are not to go down there on your own."

The tone of command reached straight past my conscious mind and into the subconscious, and I found myself nodding in agreement. I focused as best I could, swallowing and pushing back against his dominating influence.

No, I didn't let go of his hand. Would it have helped? Probably, but some sacrifices weren't worth making.

"Over a *thousand* lives are down there," I said. "We can't abandon them."

For a moment I thought Tzaron would reply, *I can.* That would be more in line with the barbarous warlord image he projected. But once more I'd underestimated him.

"Victoria-ma, they are your people. Of course we will not abandon them, but you will help no one if you fall through a patch of flooring that isn't there. I forbid you from going alone, but I will come with you and we will find your people together."

I didn't know whether to be delighted or skeptical. "You will?"

"Of course I will. If your people lie sleeping

beneath us, we will find and free them. I am no monster, Victoria-ma, and you are my mate, not my enemy."

"Now hold on there. Just because we've had sex doesn't make me your mate!"

He laughed, not unkindly, and pulled me closer. I'm sure I could have resisted if I chose to, but I'd have missed the touch of the solid blue wall of muscle that was his torso, and why would I want that?

"You are quite correct, taru-ma. The sex merely confirmed what we knew already, but I see that you have forgotten that. Perhaps you need another demonstration?"

I'm not sure what noise I made in response, but it didn't contain any words. My mind crashed to a halt as though a fuse had blown, Tzaron's words shutting down every rational thought while sending my body into overdrive.

His dark, low chuckle did nothing to help the tingling between my legs, and another tug on my hand pulled me over his lap. My heart pounded loudly enough that I half expected it to lead a rescue party to me, and I hoped they'd wait at least an hour or two. Maybe a few days.

With a soft whisper of fabric, Tzaron flipped up

my skirt. A soft slap to my ass drew a yelp from me, and I felt Tzaron's monstrous, delightful, scary cock grow against my side. Another smack, a little harder, and I arched my back, moaning.

"What are you doing?" I finally managed to ask, trying to sound outraged and failing tragically. My body trembled with the need for this man, and the spanking was more erotic than I'd expected. Oh, it hurt, but the sting blended into pleasure, a warmth that spread through me and left my breathing ragged. When Tzaron slid his hand between my legs, he pushed my panties aside and found me wet as a rainstorm.

"You know what I'm doing," he said, voice deliciously deep and soft, fingers stroking and teasing. "And all you have to do if you don't want it is tell me to stop."

I barely stopped myself from answering *'Don't you dare!'* Biting back the words, I confined myself to an enthusiastic moan, prompting Tzaron to give me another light smack on the ass before lifting me as though I weighed nothing. As he carried me across the deck, his free hand and his dexterous tail pulled my clothing from me. My blouse first, and then my skirt. My bra's fastening gave him a moment's trouble before he worked it out.

By the time he'd stripped me naked, my heart raced, and I couldn't put one thought in front of another. My naked body pressed to his bare torso, the wonderfully weird sensation of his scaled skin moving against me.

When he put me down, I whimpered and clung to him, holding tight and refusing to let go until a stronger spank convinced me. Whatever he had planned, I knew I'd love it, but letting go of him even for an instant seemed like treason to myself.

Tzaron's kilt dropped from his hips and I forgot even that thought. His hard cock pulsed as I reached out to touch it, running my fingertips up his length and enjoying his scales shifting under my fingers. His growl of lust and need made me gasp and I felt the pressure in him, the tension ready to explode.

I chewed on my lip, knowing exactly where I wanted that explosion to end up but unable to say it. Tzaron had no difficulty reading my needs, taking hold of me and turning me around. His grip was firm but gentle, too powerful to resist yet soft enough to make me feel safe in his hands.

He pushed me down across the nearest table, parting my legs as I whimpered. Hard plastic surface under me, hard alien warlord above, me trapped in between — I'd never been so happy to be confined.

My only regret was that I couldn't touch Tzaron. He laughed as I squirmed and tried to reach back for him.

Bending over me, he kissed the back of my neck, scraping his sharp teeth across my skin. "Patience, taru-ma. You will get all you need but *wait.*"

The snap of command worked wonders, freezing me in place. I almost stopped breathing. The anticipation filled me, threatened to overflow, but I stayed still as Tzaron's hands and tail roamed my body, exploring, teasing, driving me mad with lust.

His claws dragged down my flank, teeth nipped at my neck. And his tail, his wicked tail, probed between my legs, pressed against my pussy, rubbed sensually until I couldn't help myself and squirmed, arching my back.

Every inch of me trembled. My lust, my need for Tzaron's touch, for his *cock,* consumed me. I felt like I was going mad. On the verge of breaking, I looked round, ready to beg for release. The grin on Tzaron's face said that he knew how close to the edge I was, and that he could hold me here for hours if he wanted to.

Just the thought made me twitch. Hours being kept at the brink of an orgasm? I'd *die.*

As though that was the signal he'd been waiting

for, Tzaron thrust hard, driving his amazing cock deep into me. The strange, solid texture of it fitted so perfectly, as though we'd been designed for each other, and thrust after thrust slammed me against the table. I gasped with passion, each thrust driving the air from my lungs, each withdrawal leaving me moaning for more. Tzaron's growl next to my ear sent me tumbling toward orgasm. We were both lost in the moment, desperate for each other. I lost track of the point where I ended and he began, lost myself in him as he buried himself in me.

I gripped the table, knuckles white, muscles trembling, clinging to something solid. Without that, I felt like the waves of pleasure Tzaron sent through me would wash me away.

Time stopped, stood still, lost all meaning. The world faded until all I knew was me, Tzaron, and the table beneath us. Nothing else mattered. I hardly remembered that there *was* anything else. Tzaron's hands gripped tighter, his breathing ragged, and I groaned as his pace increased. He swelled inside me, stretching me deliciously. Panting and struggling not to plead with him, I squeezed back.

"Fuck, Tzaron, please, please more." Okay, I lost the struggle fast, but it's the effort that counts, right? "Harder, Tzaron, please?"

I didn't need to say more. Tzaron snarled, reached past me to grip the table and pulled himself forward with brutal, beautiful force. Both of us panted, groaned, growled as he swelled inside me and we both teetered on the brink.

Let go of all restraint.

And fell into an abyss of ecstasy that wiped the world away.

17

TZARON

What am I doing? The question sat at the back of my thoughts, nagging, as I went through the work of running my horde. Once, I'd lived for this — now every call on my attention dragged me away from my taru-ma and I resented it.

Each day, a dozen petty disputes between squabbling warbands kept me in my throne, few of them were important enough to need my judgment. It was good to know my followers relied on me, but couldn't they do it in a way that let me spend time with Victoria?

When I mentioned that to Victoria, she laughed. We took our meals in my private quarters, lounging on cushions and breathing in the thick, delightful scent that wafted from the incense burners in each corner of the room. A fine place to relax after a long day, and the only time the two of us could reliably share. Victoria sat cross-legged on the far side of the room from me. No matter how hard I glared at her, she simply laughed more.

"You know what you need, Tzaron?" she asked as she got control of her mirth. "You need to learn how to delegate. Appoint some judges who can hear those cases for you, that kind of thing. Trying to do it all yourself is impossible."

"I have managed," I said, my pride stung. "I am the leader, and they must see me pass judgment."

"On the lords, maybe, and on important questions, sure. The trouble is that you take every case yourself, and your empire's growing too big for that. It won't be long before the queue grows faster than you can answer its questions."

I grumbled at that, but she was right. "Even if I agree, what then? How do I choose judges I can trust?"

"Now that is the magic you wanted from the Vale, right? The reason you kidnapped me."

I nodded, grimacing and regulating my breathing. Victoria's smile had an edge to it, and I knew I wouldn't like whatever came next.

"I've studied Earth's history, and yes, I have some answers for you. They will cost you, though. Will you pay my price?"

"What is your price, taru-ma? I cannot agree without knowing that."

She chuckled. "I'll trust your honor, Tzaron. Promise you'll pay a *fair* price, that's good enough for me. You can judge for yourself after you've heard me out."

I chuckled at that but nodded. With anyone else, that would be a dangerously open-ended bargain. Not with me — I would never take advantage of Victoria. She knew it, too, her eyes sparkling with mischief.

She looked so infuriatingly cute, I couldn't stay angry or suspicious. Damn it.

"Okay," she continued. "There are two ways to set up a bureaucracy to run your empire. The first is probably the best but I doubt it will work for you: take your kinfolk, people you can trust because of blood ties to you. If you prosper so do they."

"My kin? I have none," I said, pulling a face. "Or rather, they are not here and that is for the best."

Victoria opened her mouth, then shook her head abruptly and closed it again. Good. There were some topics that would sour even the finest berrywine.

Instead, she pressed on. "Well, if not your kin, then how about a group you can be sure won't try to claim your throne?"

"Where would I find such paragons of virtue? Everyone wants the throne, it seems."

"Oh, they might want it, I can't speak to that. I know some who can't take it, though. None of the Zrin following you would give their loyalty to a human."

I opened my mouth, only to realize I didn't know what I wanted to say. Taking a sip of berrywine gave me a chance to rally my thoughts, and I started again.

"Beloved, you cannot take on half my duties and continue the repairs. And I doubt you would be happy if I raided for more humans and forced them to work for me. So where would be get these human bureaucrats?"

Victoria-ma grinned like a zsinz about to pounce, leaning forward. "I've told you, this vessel transported more than a thousand settlers. You have them already, you just have to go wake them up."

I blinked, taken aback. If she was right and a thousand humans slumbered in the belly of my palace, they'd be a considerable resource. If we could manage them. "Feeding a thousand extra mouths won't be easy. And how can you be sure they'll want to stay and be part of my empire?"

She shrugged. "I can't and I won't pretend I can. Probably they won't all stay, which will take the pressure off the supplies, but I figure enough will that it'll give you a core of competent humans to lessen the load. As for feeding them, there are plenty of makers aboard that can turn pretty much anything into edible mush — no one likes the stuff, but they won't starve. I've fixed up a couple of them already, to make sure they'll still work."

My heart raced, and for once it wasn't at the closeness of my mate. Well, not entirely.

"You have convinced me," I said, grabbing Victoria and pulling her to me for a kiss. "Tomorrow, we shall see about rescuing your kin."

MY TARU-MA LED me deeper into the darkness of my palace, down to where I'd never been. No light made it this far, but her companion spirit shed enough light to see by. Victoria's shoulders shook as she descended a metal staircase half-torn from the wall by the force of the crash. The stairs creaked and groaned under her weight — I didn't dare set foot on them until she made it to the decking below.

I leaped after her, hoping to be off the stairs before they realized they ought to crumple under my weight. It half-worked, the staircase coming away from the wall as I jumped clear. The metallic crash as it hit the deck behind me made me wince.

"Let's hope that there's another way back up," Victoria said, surveying the wreckage. Her nerves were showing, and I'd have sent her back up to safety if I could. Unfortunately, I knew she wouldn't go, and even if she did, I wouldn't be able to find my way in this maze without her.

It was a deathtrap, as I'd expected. Without Victoria to guide me and Count Catula to illuminate the path, I'd have fallen through damaged decking, torn myself up on the sharp edges where metal had torn, or met some equally embarrassing death. Even in her company, we'd been through plenty of close calls.

We pressed on in silence until we reached a sealed door. Nothing unusual about that, the palace was full of them, but here Victoria paused and bit her lip.

"This is where the colonists sleep?" I asked, though the answer was obvious.

"Yes," she replied, more subdued than I'd expected. Before I could ask why, she sank down into a crouch and pulled tools from her belt, prying open a mechanism and fidgeting with it. It wasn't long before the door unlocked and as soon as it did, I was there to jab a pry-bar into the gap and throw all my weight on it.

A hiss of air followed, foul-smelling and heavy with decay. I recoiled from the door, and Victoria blanched, covering her mouth and nose. Unaffected by the smell, Catula bounded forward into the room beyond, radiating blue light.

Victoria stepped hesitantly forward, spurring me into action. I wasn't about to let her go first into danger. Ducking past her I entered the room first, looking around for any foes or traps.

What I saw was a scene more fit for a horror story than anything else. Sarcophagi filled the chamber, all made of the same strange material as my palace. The 'stasis tubes' Victoria spoke of, I presumed, which made this sight all the worse. I tried to piece it together.

When the palace fell from the sky, it had struck a rock. A large one, angled just right, or maybe just wrong. A sharp edge tore through the hull, and straight through this chamber. Dozens of stasis tubes lay scattered around the vast room, wrenched from their places by the awful impact. The jagged tooth of rock that stabbed through the decking and reached to the ceiling had torn open more stasis tubes on its way through and human bodies spilled from them. I shuddered at the thought of that death. One moment asleep, the next flying through the air in agony and confusion.

"At least it was quick," Victoria said behind me. More to convince herself than me, but I did my best to take comfort from the thought.

"Did anyone survive?" I asked, my tail lashing as I looked around. No sign of life, not even vermin moving. Victoria swallowed audibly, taking tiny steps into the chamber, glancing nervously back at the door as though afraid it would slam shut and trap us with the dead.

Nonetheless, she pushed on, heading to the back of the chamber where untouched sarcophagi waited. If there were any survivors, that's where they'd be hiding.

It didn't take her long to find her answer. The

lack of lighting should have been enough of a clue, but neither of us was willing to give up hope so easily. She kept checking coffin after coffin until she ran out of them.

"No luck," she whispered, and I didn't know if she addressed me or the spirits of the dead. "The crash severed the power core, and the emergency backups didn't kick in. Those that didn't die in the impact woke in tubes that wouldn't open and stayed there till they choked on bad air or died of thirst."

"I am sorry, beloved," I rumbled. "That's an awful death."

With a shudder, she relaxed and leaned back against me. "I wish there was someone I could blame for this, you know? But it's just the cheapskates at the Arcadia Colony Company taking the lowest bidder for everything. Fuck them."

Her anger was quiet, subdued. Mine was anything but. I swung my tail, frustrated rage giving it strength, and it hit the sarcophagus on my left with an echoing thud. My claws extended of their own accord and I drew back my lips to bare my teeth, ready to sink into flesh.

Few people had the strength to face my rage, even if it wasn't aimed at them. Even close friends would freeze, try to avoid my attention, back away.

Victoria, though? She was the first to see my killing fury and step closer, putting the arms around me and holding me tight. Anyone other than my taruma would have taken their life in their hands doing that.

Not her. She would never be in danger from me. We both knew that deep in our souls.

"I will tear those miscreants apart for you," I promised, only to be silenced by a kiss.

"Hush," Victoria whispered, pulling back to look me in the eye. "They aren't even on this planet."

"Then I shall learn to fly, tack them down, and tear them into extra-small pieces," I amended, surprising myself by chuckling. "To cover the inconvenience of reaching them."

Victoria tried not to laugh, but it came out as a snort. "Tzaron! You can't joke about things like that."

"Why not? It got you to laugh, and that's what I aimed for." I lifted her against me as I spoke, turning toward the entrance. "Come, let us leave this place of tragedy. We will bury these humans with honor, send them back to the Sky Gods in good..."

I trailed off, seeing light beyond the doorway. Flickering yellows, the glow of a torch. Someone had followed us down here, against my instructions and all common sense.

Victoria felt my muscles tense, frowned and twisted in my arms, nearly escaping my grip by accident. That momentary distraction took my attention off the doorway and when I looked up there were two Zrin standing there. One held a torch aloft, the other grinned at me, bathed in that yellow glow, and I recognized him at once. Gessar.

He stood tall, no fear in his expression now, his ssav all reds and greens. And in his hands, one of the human light weapons. Almost comically small, he held it delicately — but he held it pointed at me.

"So here you are, Lord Tzaron," Gessar said almost warmly. "You should be careful wondering off on your own. Anything might happen."

I stepped in front of Victoria, instinct putting me between her and harm. Gessar laughed, his minion joining in a moment later.

"No, no, you don't understand me." Gessar's aim never wavered, even as the rest of him shook from laughing. "You don't have to worry about her safety. I'll admit I was wrong there, Tzaron — your human has proved a most valuable asset, unlocking the Sky secrets, and there are more mysteries to explore. No, it's *you* that's the problem."

"I have led the horde to power and riches," I

growled. "You are better off with me than you have ever been. And this is how you repay me?"

I inched closer as I spoke. If could get into striking range, I'd finish this at once.

Gessar's laugh was bitter, cruel, and honest. A bad sign — if he'd stopped hiding his feelings, it meant he didn't expect us to survive. "Better off? You are *smothering* me, Tzaron. Yes, my clan has riches, fine weapons, good hunting. All by your leave, not mine. Your authority, not mine. We were free, once, free to raid and loot and do as we please. Now you tell us when and who we may war on, you proclaim yourself my lord, and you think I should thank you for the honor? No. I will take your witch and let you die along with your dreams of conquest."

"You asshole," Victoria shouted from behind me. "You think I'm going to go with you? I saved your *life,* and this is the thanks I get?"

"Yes," Gessar replied. "You get spared in turn, and we're even. Though if you'd rather die with Tzaron, I suppose I can't stop you."

My growl at that made Gessar and his follower take a quick step back. Unnecessary, they were already out of lunging distance, but their fear wouldn't listen to reason.

Behind me, Victoria's silence carried as much

menace as I did. I felt it, like a deep abyss at my back, waiting to drag someone down. If she got to Gessar before I did, she'd tear him limb from limb. Or try to — fierce as my human was, I didn't rate her chances bare-handed against any Zrin.

"Calm yourselves, or I'll put you both down here and now and find myself another human to show me your magic." Gessar's grip tightened on the weapon, and I wondered how good a shot he could be with it. He couldn't have had much practice, and as deadly as those weapons were, that only mattered if he hit. And Heshra had survived being struck by a laser beam. Maybe I would be as lucky.

Hit him in a rush, and even if he did shoot a hole in me, I'd still be able to kill him before I died. I took a deep breath and braced against the metal floor.

"That threat is stupid," Victoria said, so cold I half expected frost to form around her. "You can grab another human, but they won't be able to open the datastore. It's keyed to me, and no one else can open it. You need me alive."

Gessar ground his teeth. "While you refuse to help, you are useless to me, anyway."

"So spare Tzaron." I jerked around to look at her. My beloved human standing with hands on hips and a frown on her face. Face pale, eyes blazing, she looked like an avenging goddess as she spoke. "You know what we mean to each other. Keep him alive and I'll help you with the human magic. And once I've worked for you for a year, you'll set him free and let us leave together."

"That works," Gessar said slowly, as though he was weighing the idea. I knew better — he'd find reason after reason to delay my release, and when he couldn't put it off any further, he'd 'release' me into death. "Yes, a year's loyal service and then the two of you can depart as long as you get out of my territory and don't return."

"Taru-ma," I whispered, though I didn't doubt that Gessar and his companion would overhear most of what we said. "Do not do this. You can't trust them."

She shook her head, red hair flying. "I trust them about as far as I can throw this colony pod, Tzaron-ma. But I'd rather take the risk than see you die."

"They'll keep me caged until I die, no matter what you threaten them with or what service you do them. Better an honorable death than that."

Some of the anger left her eyes, her lips twitching into an unwilling smile.

"But you'll still live longer than if you charge into laser fire," she said softly, reaching up with a small pale hand to stroke my cheek. "And perhaps the drogara will learn to sing."

Taking a deep breath, I forced down my rage and nodded. I might not agree, but she had made up her mind. And maybe the drogara *would* learn to sing.

18

VICTORIA

*T*urning my back on Tzaron and walking away was the hardest thing I'd ever done. And that was no empty phrase — I'd left my home-world and family behind, climbed into a poorly maintained spaceship. I'd woken on the wrong world and led the colonists to rebuild and make a home here, even as they resented me for bossing them around.

None of that compared to the feeling of turning my back on the alien warlord who'd kidnapped me. The man I loved.

Feelings are confusing and overrated, I told myself, as though that made any difference. *Focus on what's ahead of you, not behind.*

Two Zrin, one with a laser rifle, one with a

burning torch. Both big, well trained, dangerous. Reminding myself to breathe evenly, I approached them. Gessar didn't lift his aim from Tzaron the whole time, and as I approached, he backed away out into the corridor.

"Close the door," he hissed as soon as we were all out. I couldn't resist looking back at Tzaron, and found him looking at me, motionless. Every part of him quivered with angry energy, fighting against his self-control. He seemed on the verge of motion, vibrating and ready, but he stayed still as Gessar's bodyguard levered the heavy doors shut again.

With a dreadful *clang* that echoed through the colony pod, the locks engaged, sealing me off from my beloved. It felt as though a part of me had been cut off.

A rough shove from Gessar broke through my misery and got me moving. "How long will it take you to arm my guards with these light throwers?"

I considered the problem as he marched me through the dark corridors, trying to distract myself from the pain in my heart and the feeling that the walls were closing in.

"Tens of days, I expect." I said, trying to ignore my captor's impatient growl. "Look, I can find the armory, but the lasers are stored uncharged. We don't have the energy to charge them quickly."

I doubted he'd follow that explanation — I made no effort to use terms a Zrin would know, and we didn't have the connection Tzaron and I shared — and, as I'd expected, he didn't want to reveal his ignorance by asking. That suited me just fine.

"There must be a way to speed it up," Gessar demanded. "You are holding out on me, human."

"Well, there is one way, but it's a lot of work. The solar panels are half buried. If you and your Zrin clear the top of the ship, I'll charge the rifles for you that much quicker."

I didn't know why I told him that. This asshole with a pile of laser weapons at his beck and call sounded like the worst idea ever. He'd arm his loyalists, and then steamroller the nearby Zrin tribes, wrecking their homes and any chance of peace between humans and Zrin. Gessar would carve out an empire bigger than anything Crashland had ever seen. Unlike Tzaron, he gave zero fucks about the people he conquered, and this empire would crumble in his hands. Remembering all I'd read about the fall of empires on Earth, I shivered at the thought.

"What will you do with the lasers when you have

them?" I asked as calmly as I could. Gessar's eyes flashed as he turned toward me, instantly suspicious. Perhaps I should have waited, given him a few days to get comfortable with me working for him. Well, I'd asked now.

"It's no concern of yours, human," Gessar told me, staring as though he'd be able to see what I was hiding if he looked hard enough. A moment passed, and he continued. "I will arm my Zrin and take what is mine. A bloody tide will sweep through the caves, drowning all those who won't join me, and I will rule from a throne I craft from the corpses of my enemies."

As he ranted, the glint of suspicion in his eyes turned to a blazing inferno of rage, and I took a step back. Gessar, I realized, was quite, quite mad. He'd hidden it well, but his grievances had eaten his soul and what looked out through those eyes was a ravening beast rather than a person.

A beast that was too clever by far.

The rage vanished as quickly as it had appeared. Not gone, I knew, just hidden behind Gessar's crocodile smile. He patted my shoulder, perhaps trying to be reassuring, and continued in a more measured tone.

"You don't need to worry about that, of course.

You and I are going to be firm allies, and you will rise with me."

An alliance that will last until the moment I've taught you how to use the human technology you're interested in. I didn't say it aloud, but I thought it very hard. If either of us had been psychic, it would have been like shouting it in his face. Fortunately, neither of us were telepaths, and Gessar's attention was fully in the future, focused on his planned revenge.

"In that case, you'll want to clear that mess off the hull," I said. "So I can get your rifles ready in a hurry."

Gessar nodded and strode ahead, leaving me to scurry after him in silence until we returned to the inhabited area of the colony pod. Grisly sights greeted me as I walked — Gessar had no guide, so he'd relied on instinct to get through the maze of deathtraps the engineering levels had become. Instinct, and throwing weight of numbers at the problem.

Fresh Zrin corpses lay where they'd fallen, impaled on pipes or sliced open to bleed to death. I pictured it, Gessar and his men creeping down the passages, following us into the depths. Gessar letting his Zrin die to warn him of danger. Effective but gruesome and wasteful.

At least that means he has fewer troops to work with, I thought as I clambered past a still-twitching corpse. As silver linings went, that wasn't great.

It seemed to take forever to reach the 'safe' areas of the pod, and when we finally emerged, it was obvious that things had changed. Two of Gessar's troops guarded the doorway, and a small crowd of Zrin waited for us, muttering amongst themselves as I emerged with Gessar.

All sound ceased at his glare, and they followed us to the throne room in silence. The caged tengers hissed and growled as Gessar ascended the dais and, quite deliberately, lowered himself onto the throne. Some of Tzaron's Zrin stepped forward, reaching for their weapons as they objected, but Gessar was no fool. He'd made sure that his own warband outnumbered the loyalists in the room, and the laser rifle in his hands was its own statement of power.

"Tzaron has ceded the leadership of the New City Horde to me," he said, projecting his voice to echo off the walls. "He will be remembered as the one who united us, but the time has come to use the power he has brought us — and that task falls to me."

"Truly?" One of Tzaron's Zrin had the bravery to

resist the obvious coup. "If that's so, he would tell us himself. What have you done with him, usurper?"

The entire chamber went still, waiting on Gessar's response. My heart froze as he turned the laser over in his hands, and I wished I could think of something to say. Something to do to protect the Zrin who was so loyal to my taru-ma. Thoughts whirling through my mind, I couldn't even take a step forward in a moment that lasted perhaps five seconds but felt like it stretched on for hours.

Gessar teased out those seconds, letting tension build, before throwing his head back in a laugh that shook the room. "You are loyal to your lord, and I applaud that, even when it's misguided. Tzaron rests in meditation and he will rejoin us when he is ready to share the wisdom he has collected. If you doubt me, you are free to leave, but you will put aside the wealth we will gather in our conquests."

That lie fooled no one. Every ssav I saw in the audience showed white mixed with pale blue, and I'd learned enough to recognize those as the colors of fear and uncertainty. The only exceptions were Gessar's troops, whose ssavs turned green.

"I will not follow you, Gessar," the Zrin who'd questioned him said. "Nor will I flee like a startled gree. If Tzaron still lives, let us see him and if he backs your claims, I will serve you loyally. Until then, I will stay true to our leader and stay with his horde to find out what has really happened to him."

The sharp snap of a laser superheating the air rang out, and I winced as the red line of hot light burned a hole through the loyalist's throat. The Zrin froze. If Gessar had used a javelin, I swear he'd have been torn apart for the murder. But as far as the Zrin were concerned, the laser was a magic weapon. No one wanted to charge someone who wielded that power.

"I told him to leave," Gessar said, his voice soft and reasonable. "You all heard me, and it's true for anyone in the horde. I rule now, and if you don't like it, leave. Challenge me and join that one in death."

No one argued. Each Zrin quietly bowed before their dictator and his guards, acknowledging Gessar's usurpation.

19

TZARON

*a*s soon as the door closed behind Victoria, I sprang into action. I refused to be trapped in this charnel house while Gessar used me to force my taru-ma to work for him. Being a bargaining chip used to control the woman I loved was unacceptable.

Without Catula's glow, the room was dark as the Skyless Depths, and it took a moment to make my way across it. Once I did, I found the door sealed shut by a locking mechanism I didn't understand and had no tools to open. Hard enough to open when Victoria unlocked them for me, now they proved impossible. Feeling around the door's edge, I jammed my pry bar into the tiny gap between the door and its frame and threw all my weight against it.

Nothing changed. The doors didn't move a hair's breadth.

"Open, damn you to the Skyless Depths," I shouted, trying again, straining at the bar. Cold metal shifted under my hand and for a moment a rush of triumph filled me. It left just as quickly when I realized the bar had bent, not the doors.

"Okay, Tzaron," I spoke to myself as I summoned all my strength and braced myself. "You have faced tougher foes. Eventually all men must fail, but not here, not now, not defeated by a *fucking door.*"

I had to grin. It seemed that my taru-ma's odd linguistic habits were rubbing off, and when I saw her again, I'd never hear the end of it. That just made me even more determined to reach her. I threw myself at the pry bar, using every ounce of strength and weight, screaming at the door to move, to open.

With a terrible, echoing snap, the pry bar broke in two, sending me tumbling to the floor. I held one end of the twisted metal rod while the other fell to the deck with a clatter.

Okay, brute force wouldn't take me through the door. Going through the walls was out of the question. Every attempt to change my palace's structure had ended in miserable failure, even with teams of

Zrin and all the tools we could muster. What other options were there?

Staring into the inky blackness, I only came up with one other answer: the rock that had torn through the hull. Maybe, I thought, just maybe there was a gap large enough for me to squirm through. It was worth a try.

The carnage grew worse the closer I got, and not being able to see it only made things worse. At the far end of this giant chamber, the sarcophagi lay sealed, the bodies shut away. A terrible fate, but I hadn't seen or felt the victims. Now I walked blindly amongst scattered, decaying bodies. Dried blood underfoot, the stench of rotting meat in the air, the occasional brush against a human corpse... all conspired to make me nauseous.

Perhaps this violent death was better than waking trapped in a coffin. A shudder ran through me at the thought — I'd long ago made my peace with the painful death in battle that had been my most likely fate. But *this?* This was a horror I wouldn't inflict on my worst enemy.

Picking my way through the carnage, I made it to the rock. The stench was worst here, where dozens of coffins had torn open, spilling their human cargo over the decking. I tried not to think about it as I searched for a way out.

In the dark, it wasn't easy. The metal of the hull had warped and torn into strange shapes, like a giant sculptor had discarded his work half-finished. Some of its edges were razor-fine, which made exploring by touch slow, difficult, and sometimes painful. It took an age to circle the spike, and I did it twice before I admitted the truth to myself.

Perhaps my thumb would fit through the largest of the gaps I found, but nothing larger. Given time, I'd be able to chip away at the rock and tunnel my way out. It would take a long time, many days, perhaps a year. Far too long for me to save Victoria.

I shook my head, hefting the bent and twisted remnant of my pry bar. "Sitting here and moping won't save her. I might as well keep busy."

Sparks flew as I swung my makeshift tool into the stone.

DAYS PASSED AS I WORKED, my makeshift hammer chipping away at the rock. How many days I did not know. The only measure of time I had was the clatter of a delivery tube sending me food. I say food; it was some kind of mush that tasted like mud and stuck to my teeth. I recognized it from Victoria's description of the 'food' the maker-machines produced, and the memory of her heartened me more than the food did. It would sustain me while I dug, and it proved that Victoria still lived. If she died, Gessar would have no reason to feed me.

I had no way to know how far apart my meals were, nor even if they came on a set schedule. Four meals passed before a few of the ceiling panels lit, illuminating the horror around me in an eerie, dim light. From that point on the light never varied, giving no difference between day and night. The only measure of time passing was the progress of my work.

Distressingly slow. I'd found an escape from the trap, yes, but not a fast one. It might be years before I reached daylight, and by then Gessar would have complete control of my horde.

"This will go faster when I reach dirt," I told myself over and over, swinging my makeshift tool and chipping another fragment from the rock. Every swing, I pictured Gessar as my target. It lent strength to my arms, but even so, my words rang false. True, tunneling through dirt would be easier, but I wasn't near reaching it.

There had to be a better way. It just hadn't occurred to me yet. Victoria would have spotted it, I knew. My human mate was clever, and she had her spirit companion to advise her. I...

Wait.

A thought scratched at the edge of my awareness, like a shy animal trying to get my attention. I let my ax fall, quieted my mind, and waited. Letting it come closer at its own pace, not risking rushing it. Slowly, the idea came out into the light, and I snarled at myself. *Fool! It was right in front of me the whole time.*

I looked around the carnage until I saw a relatively intact human body. Crouching beside the dead man, I shuddered as I lifted his arm. I'd taken from the corpses of enemies I'd slain, of course, but I'd never looted a body after it was buried.

His ghost would understand, I told myself, and carefully opened his wristband's fastening. It looked like a solid silver bracelet, but when I pulled experimentally, it came apart so easily I thought I'd torn it. I breathed a sigh of relief when I saw how neat the ends were.

It barely fit around my wrist, but it did, the edges of the band sealing by some magic to leave the wristband an unbroken ring of metal once again. I paused for a moment, taking a deep breath. This might be commonplace for a human, but I had no experience of summoning spirits.

This is a day for firsts, then. I pressed my thumb on its surface as I'd seen Victoria do. The wristband vibrated, almost making me jump, and then lit up.

The spirit that appeared on my wrist looked like a bird. Mostly, anyway — perhaps this was what birds from Victoria's world were like? Only one pair of wings, feathers gray with a dusting of black, it shone with a weird inner light. It cocked its head, looking at me with eyes that held a disconcerting intelligence, then opened its beak to screech at me.

"Do you speak the Sky Tongue, spirit?" I felt foolish asking — surely a spirit that came from the sky *must* speak the language of the gods. And yet, the bird hooted again and did nothing else. Wonderful. Victoria told me the Sky Tongue wasn't widely known amongst her people, and apparently that applied to their spirits too.

The few words of the human language I'd picked up would not be enough to converse with the thing. The hope my idea had nurtured melted like snow under the summer sun and I hissed a curse at the Sky Gods for giving me that momentary idea only to snatch it away.

"I *will not* give up," I said, fierce and low. One more experiment remained to try. Doing my best to mimic human pronunciation, I pulled on my small vocabulary and spoke to the bird. "You call *Victoria Bern.* Call."

20

VICTORIA

I counted the days go by, hope draining away as they wore on. The first two weren't so bad, but on the third I wondered if Tzaron was still alive at all. Gessar's Zrin sent maker-mush down to him, and I tried to take that as a sign that he was eating the 'food' our makers could process any organic matter into. As unappetizing as the gloop tasted, it made a balanced and healthy meal — for a human. Did Zrin need something else in their diets? Would Tzaron starve, missing some vital vitamin humans didn't need?

That was my more optimistic worry. Maybe they'd gone back and killed him once I was too far away to hear. I wouldn't put it past Gessar to keep sending down food to reassure me and get as much work from me as possible before I decided my mate was dead.

Despite my fears, that day hadn't come yet. I spent my time immersed in my work, anything to keep my mind off those worries. Studying from the Vale files, I learned to trace circuits and replace the damaged parts, getting the lighting working through more of the ship. With that came more exploration, and more problems to address, and this needed a hundred of me working together. I relished the challenge, though, even though a lot of it was beyond me. It occupied my brain with something better than sitting around doing nothing but worrying.

My arms were elbow deep in a burned-out air circulator when Count Catula meowed to get my attention. It took me a moment to recognize the sound — he was flagging an incoming call for me. Which made no sense unless someone from the Vale had found the place and a rescue was in progress. Just a few days earlier, I'd have waved them off, but now my heart pounded, and a dizziness spread through me as I pulled back from the circulator and looked around at my watchdog.

Gessar wasn't willing to let me wander around on my own, and with good reason. Given unfettered access to the colony pod, I'd be able to wreak havoc on his people, but with a Zrin watching over me there was a limit to how much trouble I could get into. So there he was, a young Zrin soldier whose name I hadn't bothered to remember. Tall, skinny, and narrow-faced for a Zrin, he still had an imposing build compared to any human. There was a gangly awkwardness to his movements, like a teenager who hadn't gotten used to a growth spurt yet. It might have been endearing if he hadn't been set as my watchdog.

Lucky for me, my work was boring to watch. On the second day, the guard had started looking for ways to pass the time as I worked on problems he had no way to understand. Today, he leaned against the wall, talking quietly with a female Zrin who hung on his every word, wide-eyed. God, I hoped they weren't going to fuck. I did not need to see or hear that, but the way they touched each other made it a distinct possibility.

Don't know what she sees in him, but if she's distracting him, I'll take it. I tapped my wristband to accept the call.

"Torran?" I whispered. Who else would lead a rescue mission into the heart of a Zrin horde? The Prytheen warrior was braver than was good for him and he felt he owed me a favor.

So it shocked me beyond words when a low hissing voice answered. "Vicky-ma, you live."

"Tzaron-ma?" I hesitated, biting my lip, not believing the evidence of my senses. Catula projected the call data in floating green text and my mouth went dry as I understood. According to the colony database, I was being called by Januk Ingolmann, winner of the colony lottery. *Some prize you won, friend.*

One moment Januk had been alive and well in Earth orbit. But once the stasis tube's door shut... nothing. And now Tzaron had his companion AI.

"Thank the Sky Gods," my alien mate hissed, a crackle of static nearly drowning out his voice. The communicator relays were on my list to fix, but I hadn't prioritized them. Why bother when I was the only one with a communicator for miles around? Now I wished I'd fixed them first and ignored such things as air circulators and water purifiers.

"How did you—" I cut myself off. I didn't need to know how he'd gotten the bracelet. What mattered was that we could talk, and that meant we still had a chance. "Never mind that, are you all right?"

"I am. More importantly, are you?" The underlying rage in his voice was clear, like a tidal wave of blood looming high and waiting for the chance to crash down on whoever threatened me.

"Yes, I'm unhurt," I said, and felt the immediate threat of an explosion subside. "Gessar hasn't been a good employer, but he's feeding me enough and letting me rest when I need to. I guess he's realized my value as a 'magician' because god knows there's no other reason to."

"No," Tzaron said, voice hard as iron. "He knows nothing of your value. He wants parlor tricks from you, but you are so much more than the magic you know. It took me too long to see what a wonder you are, Vicky-ma, and I will *not* allow you to doubt it."

My cheeks burned and I didn't know where to look. Thank fuck we were talking over the communicators — if I'd been in his presence, I don't know what I would have done. Melted from embarrassment, probably, or thrown myself at him. At least with half the ship between us, I could keep my emotions under control.

"I, ah, that is, um," I said. *Oh, real smooth Vicky. Yep, emotions totally under control.*

"We must speak of our counterattack," Tzaron said, throwing me a lifeline. I grabbed hold with both hands, hauling myself out of the torrent of confused thoughts and feelings to something more practical.

"Escape first, right?" I asked. He couldn't mean to take on all of Gessar's forces at once, not on his own. That would be madness.

"Escape?" A dark low laugh echoed through the communicator and I winced. "No, my love. If we escape, I surrender the horde to Gessar and will never reclaim it. I gather the Zrin together because we will need to protect ourselves in this new world you and the Prytheen have brought from the Sky. Gessar wants to wield it as a hammer, for revenge against those who wronged him."

I opened my mouth to argue, then shut it without a word. Tzaron was right. If we let Gessar have his way he'd wreck every Zrin city he could reach, and probably every human or Prytheen one too. We couldn't just leave and let that happen.

If for no other reason, the Vale was far too close to his headquarters for safety. *Okay then. Madness it is.*

"We can't fight alone," I objected. "If we leave, we can come back with reinforcements. We're more likely to stop him that way."

I didn't expect Tzaron to accept that, but he paused. I could just imagine his face, brows furrowing as he thought, and restraining my giggles at that thought wasn't easy.

"It would be easier with help," he agreed. "You will escape back to your people, and I will stay here to fight. With your flying machines, you'll be back to reinforce me and together we'll destroy Gessar."

I blinked at that, surprised. "No way. Nope. I'm staying with you, whatever you do. I'm not about to run off and fetch some soldiers, only to come back and find you dead. Besides, I'd never make it back to the Vale on my own."

Another chuckle, and I realized he'd been teasing me. Fucker. He knew as well as I did that I wouldn't abandon him. Just like I knew he wouldn't retreat.

"First things first," I said, leaving the *you asshole* unspoken. "If we can't get you out of there, we won't organize anything."

I sat back against the cold metal wall and thought. Getting down to Tzaron was out of the question — my guard ignored me for now, but even he'd notice if I tried to get past him. And then there were more guards to worry about on the way down. No, the direct way was too risky.

But it wasn't *me* that needed to get down to the transport bay, it was Count Catula. He was the one with the code to unlock the door and release Tzaron. Could I get the wristband down to him? Maybe if I got it into Tzaron's portion of maker-goop, but I didn't know the schedule. Besides, the wristband was too easy to notice.

Count Catula mewed quietly and headbutted my hand. Absently, I scratched his head, then frowned. It was too easy to forget that he was an AI sometimes, and I'd let myself fall into that trap.

"Tzaron-ma, how did you get that wristband to call me?"

"I imitated the sounds you make to yours," Tzaron replied. "It responded. Why?"

"Okay, I'm going to need you to repeat exactly what I say to it. I can send it the language files so it'll understand Sky Tongue, and share my access codes. You'll be able to ask it to open the doors, and anything else."

It took several tries to get through to Januk's companion AI. Tzaron's mouth, kissable though it was, couldn't quite fit itself around the words I spoke. But that never discouraged my darling Zrin, who worked and worked until he mimicked my words well enough for the AI to accept the commands.

Catula purred as the files started transferring

across, then faded away in a shimmer of blue-black light. The file transfers filled the bandwidth between Tzaron's communicator and mine, making conversation impossible.

I sighed, realizing too late that Tzaron hadn't settled on the rest of the plan. I knew what he'd say, though. Get to somewhere safe, wait for him to reach me. Don't take any chances.

A grin crept onto my face, and I kicked shut the panel I'd been working on. Yes, Tzaron would have told me to do that, but he hadn't. Which meant I wasn't going against his plan if I took a chance to help...

The clatter of the panel swinging shut drew my guard's attention, much to his companion's disgust.

"What are you doing, human?" he snarled, eyes narrowed and tail swishing from side to side.

"Finished here," I lied, pretending to consult my to-do list. Several more air circulators needed my attention, but I had no intention of wasting my time on those. They could wait. "Next on my list is alpha section, port three."

The guard's glare intensified and for a moment I thought I'd pressed too hard. But his companion spoke next, and as soon as she did, his angry expression lifted. I hid a smile — the young lovers were frustrating to watch, but their skewed priorities served my purpose this time.

I just hoped they'd be distracted enough to not realize where we were headed until it was too late.

I'D NEVER BEEN in this part of the palace before, though the layout was identical to the Vale megapod. The designers intended it to be a residence for essential workers, and that's how we used ours, but the rooms were tiny for Zrin. Cramped for humans, the towering aliens would have an uncomfortable stay.

An odd place for a Zrin warband to settle, but it was also defensible, with only one way in. I didn't see any guards posted at the entrance, but a bright red line painted across a doorway marked the border, Zrin writing behind it. My guard hissed and stopped. He'd realized where I was taking him.

"We cannot go in there," he said, grabbing my shoulder to hold me back. "It's forbidden."

I tsked, turned to look at him, and rolled my eyes where I was sure his girlfriend would see. "I guess you can tell Gessar why his water's coming through full of grit and decaying vermin, then. He'll understand, I'm sure."

He didn't rise to the bait. Maybe there was more to him than just a horny teenager, after all. "You'll have to work that out with Lord Gessar. My duty is to keep you safe, in one piece, and working. Which I can't do if you cross that line and get slaughtered by the scouts."

Damn it, he's being altogether too reasonable. I tried to push harder, making myself laugh. "What, is the big and mighty Zrin warrior afraid?"

He bristled at that, waves of red washing through his ssav. But still he maintained his control, and I had to admit a grudging respect for Gessar's choice of guard.

To my relief, his girlfriend stepped in to egg him on. "Come on, Zariax, you're not scared of the scouts, are you? You have the overlord's blessing, no one will stop you."

Watching his reaction would have been amusing in any other situation. Torn between impressing his girl and following his orders to keep me safe, his face and ssav went through a range of expressions, from joy to fear to stoic acceptance.

"I am *not* afraid," he said through gritted teeth. "It's the right thing to do, that's all. Then I can come back here with proof that Lord Gessar commanded this."

"Big brave warrior," I taunted, glad that I wasn't a Zrin. If I had a ssav, they'd have seen just how frightened I was, how much I felt was riding on it. But even Tzaron had a hard time reading my emotions, bless him. Other Zrin stood no chance. "What are you so scared of, Zariax?"

His growl filled the corridor, and the blood drained from my face. I managed to cross my arms to hide the shiver of fear that ran through me, and I kept my eyes on his.

"You won't hurt me, Zariax," I told him, voice steady and light, as though his threat amused me. "Gessar would string you up with your own entrails if you lay a finger on me."

His girlfriend took that moment to remind me that she wasn't on my side. "Are you going to let the human szorc-spawn speak to you like that?"

Crap. Overplayed my hand. Well, I'm here now, better make the best of it.

Zariax raised a hand, claws emerging from his fingers as he snarled. "I can't kill you, human. That doesn't mean I can't hurt you — as long as you can still walk, anyway."

Talking had gotten me into this mess, but it

wouldn't get me out. Time to try something different. I kicked Zariax in the shin, hard as I could, and twisted out of his loosening grip as he roared in pain. Off balance, my lunge toward the doorway was more of an undignified scramble, and I had no illusion that Zariax wouldn't catch up in seconds. That had to be enough time.

Passing the red line, I threw myself forward into the scouts' lair, screaming for help. A vice-like hand closed on my ankle, dragging me back, and I twisted around to kick at Zariax. He fended off my feeble attack with ease, clawed hand rising to strike—

—and freezing in midair.

I let out a trembling breath and looked round. We had an audience, three Zrin with spears leveled at Zariax.

"You have crossed the line," one of them said. I recognized the voice — Jokzar, Heshra's guard. I'd spoken with him in medbay, and he'd seemed nice as long as he wasn't threatening me. With any luck, he remembered our conversation fondly.

"A misunderstanding," Zariax replied. "Lord Gessar commanded—"

"Your Lord Gessar doesn't command here. This is scout territory. That was the deal with Tzaron, and

Gessar swore to uphold it. Leave now and do not return."

"Of course, yes, thank you." I'd never heard a Zrin sound so relieved. "I'll take this one and go."

Gripping my ankle, he stood and began dragging me over the border again. Before I could come up with a plan to get out of his grip, Jokzar slammed the butt of his spear into the decking.

"The human stays."

"What? No, she is Lord Gessar's property. I apologize if she disturbed you, but I have to bring her back."

Jokzar looked from him down to me, then back. "She doesn't want to go, it seems. Leave her, and we'll see what value your lord sees in her."

Zariax dropped my leg and I scrambled toward Jokzar, deeper into scout territory.

"If she's going with you, so am I," Zariax said. He didn't look happy about that, not one bit "Or you can kill me for following my duty, I suppose."

Brave or stupid, the kid's loyalty was impressive. I hoped he lived to exaggerate this story for his girlfriend. Jokzar looked as impressed as I was and nodded. "You may come, but I'll give no assurance of your safety."

With that, the three scouts turned and led us into their lair.

The only room big enough to hold an audience was still tiny compared to the meeting hall where Tzaron and now Gessar held court. Heshra had done what she could with it, bright hangings giving the illusion of space and soft lighting making it look more luxurious than it was. A few scouts sat around, talking or gambling, until they saw us entering. Once we were in the room, everyone focused on us.

The warlord herself lounged on a pile of cushions in place of a throne, and she reminded me of a big cat. Appropriate, I was in the lion's den now, and I had to hope she'd remember me fondly for healing her.

And not dwell on the fact that I'd shot her in the first place.

"What have we here, Jokzar?"

While the scout reported our arrival, Heshra looked me over, then Zariax, and then back to me. Waving Jokzar to silence, she pointed at Zariax next. "You. What is your side of this story?"

"I am here under orders of Lord Gessar, to guard the human and make sure it doesn't get into trouble — or get any ideas about escape."

"Not doing a great job, are you?" Heshra snorted,

and a glance at Zariax's ssav showed the mix of fear, shame, and anger rushing through him. But again, he did better than I'd expected and refused to rise to the bait.

"No, I am not. I expect Lord Gessar will have words for me when I return, but that is still why I'm here. I will take the human back to Gessar, or you will kill me and start a war you cannot win."

Heshra grinned and nodded, then turned to me. And it all came pouring out, Gessar's betrayal. Tzaron trapped below. Our need for help. Once I'd started speaking, I couldn't stop. It was all I could do to hold back the fact that Tzaron was planning his own attack *now*.

When I ran out of steam, all eyes were on me. My story stammered to a halt and silence fell on the room.

"Why should we get involved?" Heshra asked after a long pause. I had to admit that was a valid question. Holding my head up, I looked her dead in the eye.

"Because Tzaron values your skills, and Gessar doesn't." I said, hoping I'd read the situation right. "If Gessar keeps control, he won't thank you. He's working to put his loyalists in every position of power, and you aren't one of them. Tzaron, though? He already knows how valuable you and your scouts are, and if you stick with him when he needs you he'll remember that."

Part guesswork, part knowledge of Earth history. Dictators like Gessar propped themselves up by surrounding themselves with sycophants, and whatever Heshra's faults, that wasn't one of them. Did they do the same here? I didn't know, and I didn't dare stop to acknowledge that. Keep talking, sound confident, don't let them see the panic-sweat or the trembling legs. It had worked back in Vale, and it would work here.

It had to, because I had no more tricks.

Heshra, lounging on her throne of cushions, cocked her head and grinned. Sharp teeth gleamed, but the expression didn't reach her eyes. "Ah, and you can speak for Tzaron in this? You can *promise* a reward worth the risk? In case you hadn't noticed, human, the odds are against your lord whichever side I choose. It would be safer for me to tell Gessar what you two are planning and get some credit with him that way."

I swallowed, looking into her impenetrable eyes. No hint of mercy, no shred of empathy. I might have been looking into the depths of space for all I could read from her. *Screw it. Full ahead and damn the engines.*

"It would be safer," I agreed. "You're right, Heshra, that would be the *safe* move. You might be mentioned in the histories, a minor footnote, a story about the virtues of not taking risks."

Something sparked in Heshra's eyes and she sat forward, almost ready to pounce. Around us, her scouts murmured and snarled. I had their attention, now to use it before they murdered me.

"Or you could go a different way and be remembered forever as the warlord who dared to defy injustice despite the odds. Who stood by her chosen leader when all else abandoned him and overthrew the usurper who'd taken his throne."

Some of her Zrin slapped their tails against the floor in what I chose to assume was applause, and Heshra looked around at them before replying.

"What if you've misjudged me, and I don't think the risk is worth it? Perhaps I turn you over to Gessar anyway."

"In that case, I die, Gessar kills Tzaron, and you get a pat on the head," I told her, hoping she couldn't hear the stress in my voice or my heart hammering in my chest. "But you won't. I know you too well to believe it.

You were the first over the ultrasonic fence at the Vale, leaping headlong into laser fire and across a moat of terror. Then you chased a human with a rifle, and—"

"—and you shot me," Heshra interrupted. I winced but pressed on.

"I've not known you long, Heshra, but in that time you've never taken the easy way out of a problem. Not when there's a crazy, stupid, awesome way to take instead, and damn the odds. You're like Tzaron in that, so I'm sure you'll do the *right* thing now, not the *easy* thing."

Heshra stared at me, evaluating, and I clamped my fingers painfully on my arms to keep myself from shaking. At last she threw back her head and laughed before throwing herself onto her cushion-throne.

"Tzaron and I aren't the only ones, are we, human? You are one for grasping at mad chances rather than giving in, too."

I shook my head, but my glowing red cheeks told a different story and there was no point in pretending. "Fine, yes, this is my last-ditch gamble. If you don't help, Tzaron-ma will be on his own."

Heshra laughed, thumping her soft throne with her hands. My jaw clenched and my eyes narrowed, and my face would have flushed if it hadn't already glowed red.

"Not laughing at you," Heshra said before I could pull myself together enough to say something stupid. "But you are so wrong it's funny. Whether or not I join you, Tzaron will never be alone while you are in his pack."

The air hung heavy around me as I waited. And waited. The strange bird-spirit sat frozen in mid-air, surrounded by a circle of white light. As I watched, blue poured slowly in, filling the circle from the bottom. A timer, I realized, the blue following around the circle like water flowing around a pipe. It seemed my companion wouldn't do anything while the information Vicky-ma sent me settled in.

I no longer needed to focus on digging through rock, but that was a spear with two points. It meant rest, yes, but also seeing the devastation around me. I almost wished for the darkness to return. At first I prowled up and down the massive chamber, too emotional to stay still. Rather than waste that energy,

I turned it to some use, looking for something to use as a weapon.

A torn strip of metal from the pod's hull proved perfect. One end broad and sharp, the other thin enough to grip easily, it made a satisfying swish as I swung it through the air. A crude ax, but there were no points for style in a war.

The dagger hanging from my belt was probably a better weapon — crafted by a skilled smith, honed to a razor's sharpness, well balanced and familiar. But there was something about the shard of heavy, unknown metal. Something that called to me, a roughness to match my soul.

"No one loses a battle by bringing a spare weapon," I growled aloud, though there was no one I needed to justify myself to.

Wearying of my pacing, I stopped by the door and sat down to wait, looking around the room and trying not to focus on that infuriatingly slow progress circle. There were details I had paid no attention to earlier, pictures hanging on the walls of the chamber, showing a strange and alien world in vivid color.

The longer I looked, the less plausible those images looked. How could someone paint something like that? The detail was incredible, beyond anything I'd seen. It was like looking through a window into the bizarre forest beyond. *Green* trees? Captions written across the pictures might explain the strangeness, but while I'd learned a few words of the humans' spoken language, their alphabet remained a mystery.

"That must be an image of the Arcadia Vicky-ma spoke of," I said aloud, my voice swallowed by the giant room. Had they kept these icons out of religious awe, to remind them of what waited for them after their long sleep? Each picture showed a different scene, all beautiful in their surreal way. Here, two humans held hands, children playing behind them. There, a woman stood at the top of a mountain looking down at a building surrounded by neatly defined fields. Everywhere, happy humans embraced a world empty of the dangers they'd found here.

Surrounded by dead pilgrims who would never even know they'd missed their target, I sat in silence and allowed myself to grieve for them. They'd been brave enough to leap between the worlds, along with my taru-ma. And those who had woken here were fierce enough to take on a world they didn't know, one far more dangerous than they'd prepared for, and stake a claim of their own.

That was worthy of respect. I sighed, a heavy feeling in my stomach. Why did this have to be complicated? Could I not have an enemy unworthy of sympathy?

Cheer up, Gessar is a vicious, short-sighted traitor. No complexity there, he's threatened my taru-ma and will die for it. If I ever get out of this room.

As though on cue, the hologram sprung to life with a high-pitched shriek that chilled the blood.

"Can you understand me now?" I asked warily. It nodded and spread its wings, flapping closer to grab hold of my arm. The spirit's talons bit into my skin, a ghostly touch I barely felt, and wide eyes stared at me. In their depths I saw movement, images shifting and blurring with one another, human writing flicking past. A mesmerizing display, if not an informative one.

"Let me try that again," I said, enunciating my Sky Tongue words clearly. "Do you understand?"

The bird nodded quickly, and I breathed a sigh of relief. "Good. Then open the door."

Its head twisted to one side as though wanting to ask a question, so I pointed out the door in question. The bird-spirit rotated its head to follow my gesture, twisting so far I thought its neck would snap. Vicky-ma's 'Earth' held strange creatures indeed.

For a moment I feared the spirit was as stupid as it was strange. Then it screamed, a loud and awful sound which almost covered the clicking of the locks. Released, the door slid open a hand's breadth before grinding to a halt again. That made prying it the rest of the way open easier — I pushed the doors just far enough apart to squeeze between them, and then I was free of the dreadful chamber of horrors. Free to hunt my prey.

THIS PART of my palace was unfamiliar, hardly explored. This was the only trip I'd made so far down, and I'd taken it days ago. Finding my way back up would be a challenge, but one that I'd overcome. I had to, for Victoria's sake. When I didn't remember which way to turn, I followed my instincts and hoped they'd lead me to my taru-ma.

I didn't know if it was my imagination, but the bond between us seemed strong enough to follow, as though a physical link fastened my heart to hers. Following that connection, I made my way through the darkness lit only by Screech. It might not be the best name for my new spirit companion, but I had to call him something. He screeched, so Screech he would be.

I sent him soaring ahead, watching the area he illuminated and looking for danger. There was plenty to find — huge rents in the floor left dangerous drops into the dark below, sharp metal twisted into deadly spikes. The damage I couldn't see proved a greater risk, though.

That was nearly the last thing I ever learned. My foot came down on a section of flooring which looked no different from any other, but as soon as I put my weight on it I heard the dreadful sound of metal tearing. My reflexes kicked in, sending me tumbling back rather than forward, and I crashed to the floor, heart pounding.

Approaching the place where I'd nearly fallen through, I saw a gap where the floor panel had given way. My weight had been too much for it and peering through the opening, I saw why. The level below was in chaos, gutted and mangled by the crash, and the supports were wrecked, fire-damaged, or torn loose from the walls. Trying to walk across that would be suicide.

Backtracking and finding a way around the damage might have been the best course of action. We'd come down without passing this way, so all I needed to do was retrace my steps. But I balked at the idea of losing any more time to this maze of corridors and shadows, and my instincts told me to press on. The link to my taru-ma, real or imagined, tugged me onward down this corridor, and with every passing second my sense of urgency increased.

"You cannot help her if you are dead," I reminded myself in my sternest tones. It didn't help — all of my life, all of my successes, had come from grasping opportunities no matter the risk. Playing safe now, when Vicky's life was on the line... no.

As a compromise, I told Screech to contact her again, but there was still no response. I growled, gathering myself and looking at the damaged patch of floor. If Vicky-ma wasn't answering, it meant she needed to be rescued. Or avenged.

Rescue got less likely by the second, and revenge was a hollow prospect. Killing Gessar wouldn't bring her back if he'd slain her. I had to reach them first. Crouching like a hunter about to pounce, I took a few deep breaths and offered a prayer to the Sky Gods before launching myself into a leap over the hidden abyss, hoping I'd judged the distances right.

Everything seemed to move in slow motion, as though I had hours, *years,* to think about the choices that had brought me to this point. A great and terrible rise to power, starting as a slave and ending here, in my palace, falling to my death trying to leap a chasm on a hunch.

My life passed before my eyes, and the high points were all Vicky. My first sight of her through the dust clouds, grim defiance in every line of her being. Saving her from the jungle when her escape attempt blundered into a nest of kzor. The way she'd reacted when I pinned her to the ground, and the feel of her lips on mine.

I could not, would not, fail her.

The metal flooring struck me like a hammer, and I rolled to absorb the impact. Though the floor creaked ominously under me, it held. I'd been right. With a muttered prayer of thanks, I picked myself up and turned the corner to see the wreckage of the stairs Vicky and I had descended what felt like a lifetime ago. The damaged remains protruding from the wall would do for hand holds to climb. Pulling my lips back in a snarl I began my ascent, seeking my prey.

As I APPROACHED the explored regions of my palace, I slowed and told Screech to keep himself hidden.

He obligingly faded away into thin air, and I shivered. Having a spirit like this at my command was like something from the old tales.

But his light had seen me through the darkness below, and for that he would have my perpetual gratitude. Now I no longer needed his light. The flicker of flames shone through a doorway ahead and I heard muttering voices beyond.

"—not saying he's wrong, Hrozar," a Zrin said. I couldn't place the voice, but it had been a long time since my horde got too big for me to know everyone in it.

"You are, Zarjk," another answered, exasperated and sharp. "So shut up before someone else hears you, someone who'll tell Lord Gessar about your questions."

"All I want to know is, if Tzaron's so safely locked up, why are we guarding the door to where he's kept?"

"Sky Gods' guts and entrails, idiot. We're here to make sure no one's going to go down there and let him out. And we're doing it because Lord Gessar said to and neither of us want to find out what happens if we disobey him."

I guessed these two had been comrades a long time, their bickering friendly and formalized. More relevant was the confirmation that they were guarding against someone going down the stairs, not someone coming up them.

Tuning out their words, I crept up to the doorway. Despite their apparent ill-discipline, both Zarjk and Hrozar kept their attention focused on where they thought any threat would come from — the palace itself. They didn't notice me until I stood between them, and then only because I spoke.

"One chance, friends. Stay loyal to the horde and you'll be my friends. You don't want to choose to be my enemies."

Under less pressing circumstances, I'd have enjoyed the emotions that showed on their ssavs. Horror, surprise, shock, all trying to show themselves, tendrils of white, red, and amber twining around each other. But their reflexes were well trained, and no matter what emotions showed on their skins, it didn't slow them. Both reached for their knives in the same moment, and that was the sign I'd waited for. My claws sliced left, opening Zarjk's throat, and my tailspine stabbed up into Hrozar's brain with a sickening squelch. Both bodies slumped to the floor silently, leaving me with an emptiness in my heart where the joy of battle ought to be.

They might be rebels, they might have declared for the man who wanted to kill me and my mate, but they were still warriors of the horde, still sworn to my service and killing them was different from killing external enemies. Every Zrin of the horde who died in this conflict would be a life wasted.

Though I didn't like it, I had no alternative. Not unless I wanted to surrender to Gessar, which I refused to do. I shoved the two corpses in the dark corridor I'd emerged from, far enough back that they wouldn't be spotted straight away. Blood trails made the hiding place obvious, but this might buy me a few heartbeats' time, and the throne room wasn't far.

I crept closer, taking the smaller side passageways rather than walking into Gessar's guards. They'd be watching every entrance into the throne room proper, but the closer I got before the alarm went up, the more chance I'd have.

As I got closer, I heard voices ahead. Mostly one voice, shouting and accusatory — Gessar, unhappy with his subordinates? I couldn't help smiling at that. Let him see that leadership wasn't easy, that getting to the top was only the first step of ruling. Perhaps not the easiest, but certainly less complicated than keeping a grip on the horde.

And his tantrum gave me a valuable distraction, letting me get closer than I should have before being spotted. A guard stood at the door to the throne room, but his attention was on the drama inside. My smile widened into a feral hunter's grin and I crept closer.

I hadn't paid attention to what Gessar was so enraged by. It could have been any one of the dozens of disputes he'd deem beneath him. I ignored him, focusing on creeping closer, until he spoke one word that drew my full attention.

"—human, I will take your head for this. I'll throw you to zsinz, let them tear the flesh from your bones while you're still alive to feel it, and I'll make your precious Tzaron watch." His rage-filled voice echoed, and there could only be one human he'd threaten like that. Suddenly cautious, I held very still and listened. Striding in at the wrong moment would just get Victoria-ma killed. I would not be responsible for that.

Two paces ahead of me, the inattentive guard made a disgusted noise. His attention was fully on the throne room, and he didn't like what he saw. *Tough, that's who you chose to follow. If you want to survive it, you need to take a stand against Gessar now.* I had no sympathy for those who chose an awful leader just because he said things they liked to hear.

"You can kill me any time," Vicky said, and I forgot the guard completely in my desire to shake her. *Don't remind him of that!* "But if you kill me, who will get those laser rifles working? The ones you promised your loyal followers? I think you still need me."

"My Zrin will do as they are told. I am the leader!"

"Oh, they'll obey you about as well as you obeyed Tzaron-ma," she replied, and I marveled at her cool, calm, controlled voice. The silence that followed her words was deafening.

Gessar was a fool for letting her talk. My Vicky-ma knew what she was about, and in a war of words she'd leave him bleeding from a thousand fatal wounds. Unfortunately, he could kill her with a single command, and would as soon as he realized he wouldn't win any other way.

"He was not a real leader, not like I am," Gessar spluttered, and Vicky laughed. I heard a few gasps of shock from around the room, memorized their location, counted them. It sounded like the throne room was full again. This fight wouldn't be easy, and it would come down to whose side the audience took.

Which meant that Vicky-ma's performance would be as important to the outcome as mine. My heart warmed at the thought. If I had to place my life and success in the hands of another, hers were the only hands I'd trust.

"Tzaron-ma would never be a leader like you, no," she continued, and I knew she'd be wearing that infuriatingly cute half smile that drove me crazy. "No, Tzaron kept his promises, kept the peace between the clans, and listened to all of those who followed him. Nothing like you, Gessar. He treated leadership as a responsibility, you treat it as a prize."

Those words were a slap Gessar couldn't ignore. I didn't need to see him to know how he'd react, and I didn't know if Vicky-ma had a plan past this point beyond dying gloriously. Even dying, she might have dealt Gessar's leadership an unrecoverable blow — but that wasn't worth the sacrifice, not to me.

22

VICTORIA

The meeting hall looked different with Gessar on the throne. Guards lined the walls, ready to deal with anyone who defied his rule. More surrounded him, keeping him separate from his Zrin subjects — treating them as petitioners coming to beg his favor rather than people he owed protection to. The contrast to Tzaron's rule couldn't have been starker.

Behind that line of guards stood Krosak, awkward and embarrassed. His new sash marked him as the commander of the guard, though he didn't look happy at the promotion. *Your thirty pieces of silver not enough to salve your conscience? Tough luck.* As Tzaron's deputy, he'd been the only Zrin who knew where we'd gone. The only one who could have sold us out to Gessar. I wasn't inclined to sympathy.

Gessar looked like he'd woken up this morning and decided to wear every valuable thing he owned. It looked ridiculous, but it made clear how much wealth he had to hand out. Not a bad tactic, even if he needed an image consultant. Beside him, flanking the throne, were Sorcha and Kyrix. The pair of tengers lay in cages, and I wondered what unlucky bastards had been tasked with locking them up.

The usurper's lips pursed as he looked at me, red rushing into his ssav, his knuckles white on the arms of the throne. Heshra's grip on my wrists tightened and I winced in pain, but otherwise ignored her.

We stood in the center of a circle, Zrin surrounding us. Some were shocked, others looked scared, and a few were watching with undisguised interest. Did they want to see what I was up to? Or were they just keen to see my blood spilled? No way of knowing.

It reminded me too much of a council meeting, dozens watching, no one willing to step up and speak. Regardless of how they felt about Gessar's coup, they preferred to keep silent so they could claim to be on the winning side once things settled.

That kind of equivocating was nothing new to me. I'd seen it all my life, from PTA meetings to the Vale colony's council. From the look of him, this was Gessar's first experience of it — now that he met pushback, his 'loyal followers' were a lot less eager to back him up. He didn't like it one bit.

"Bring her here," Gessar snarled into the awkward silence. "I'll show you all what happens to those who defy me."

Heshra shoved me forward before I made a sarcastic response, walking me toward the throne. I swallowed, prayed without knowing what I was praying for, and the line of guards parted ahead of me. Gessar stood, the two caged tengers flanking the throne howling eerily as I came closer. *Yes, girls, hello, I'm glad to see you too.*

They didn't look like they'd eaten in a week, and I doubted they'd been out of their cages since I'd seen them last either. But still, they recognized me and I wondered if Gessar throwing me to the pair would work out the way he wanted. Would starvation overcome their affection? It hardly mattered. Too angry for any kind of clever execution, Gessar would tear my head from my shoulders or something simple and brutal like that.

Remembering to take deep, even breaths, I

approached the throne. If I was to die at his hand today, then at least I'd die making an impression on the audience. Not the best way for this to go, but the only one I had control over.

The room fell silent as Gessar glared at me. There was no way any of us could miss the thump of a falling body and all heads turned to see a guard in a pool of his own blood. Over him, looking calm and collected, stood Tzaron.

Blood dripped from his claws, though his ssav showed not a hint of red. Icy blue lines made a complex pattern against his darker blue skin, and his eyes burned with a passion as he looked at Gessar, Heshra, and me.

"Gessar," he hissed into the silence that filled the room. "You are sitting in my chair. Up. Now."

The crack of command in his voice got Gessar half out of the throne before he realized he was obeying his enemy, and I couldn't help smirking — not that I'd have been able to resist. The sheer power my mate's voice had over me made my head swim and a tingle of desire ran through me despite the danger we were in. If Heshra hadn't tightened her grip on my wrists, I'd have thrown myself at Tzaron then and there, and most likely gotten us both killed.

Straightening up, Gessar snarled. "I rule now, Tzaron. You betrayed the horde when you sided with the human and I will not sully my claws with your blood. Guards, kill him."

At that, things happened too fast for me to follow. Tzaron sank into a crouch, ready for a final attack on Gessar despite the guards arrayed between them. Around the room, a dozen guards stepped away from the wall, lowered their spears, and advanced on Tzaron.

Gessar was taking no chances, despite the numbers. He lifted a laser rifle from beside the throne, and my blood ran cold.

And Heshra? She whistled a low note, like a bird mourning its lover.

Behind the advancing guards, her scouts appeared as though from nowhere. They'd lurked in the shadows and the crowd, their ssavs blending in like perfect camouflage in the smoke-filled room. The attack was brutal, and I'd have felt sorry for them if they hadn't been about to murder Tzaron. Gessar howled at the treachery, raising his laser but Heshra didn't give him a chance to use it. She leaped on the laser rifle, tearing it from Gessar's hands and tumbling to the deck with it clutched to her chest.

Guards closed around her, trying to wrestle it free or at least stop her from using it.

Tzaron must have been as surprised by this turn of events as Gessar, but he showed no more shock than a statue would. Fearless and implacable, he advanced on Gessar. The two leaders locked eyes as the room dissolved into chaos around them, Zrin turning on each other in the name of one leader or the other.

A guard, one not ambushed by Heshra's scouts, lunged at Tzaron. With dreamlike slowness, my alien lover swung his arm out, striking the spear just behind the razor-sharp tip and knocking it aside. The guard's momentum carried him forward, into reach of Tzaron's other hand which met his throat hard. The rushing attack turned into a graceless tumble and the Zrin didn't rise again.

"Send no more children to do a man's work," Tzaron shouted, his voice cutting through the chaotic din of the melee. "Face me, Gessar, or show your followers what a coward you are."

Gessar's response was to prove the accusation of cowardice true. Rather than attacking Tzaron, he grabbed me by the throat, sinking his claws in hard enough to draw blood. The pain knocked me out of my state of shock, but it was too late to resist. He'd crush my throat before I did anything, and even if I did pull free, his claws would keep half of my neck.

"Surrender, Tzaron," Gessar bellowed. Where Tzaron's voice projected strength, that shout held desperation. "Surrender, and you can leave with your female. Fight, and even if you win, your only prize will be her corpse."

As though to make his point, he shook me by the neck and I couldn't help whimpering. My eyes fixed on Tzaron, trying to tell him not to take the deal. Gessar would kill him the moment he had a chance. Maybe me too. Or he might be stupid enough to keep me around for my 'magic' in which case I'd find a way to kill him, though that would be a hollow victory without Tzaron.

I needn't have worried. Tzaron's dashing grin was all the reassurance I needed — he was going to try something sneaky. I just had to be ready to react, which was easier said than done, given that I didn't know what was coming.

Gessar shook me again. "I'll crush her throat and you can watch her choke to death if you don't do as you're told, Sky Gods curse you."

Tzaron's response was to throw his arm forward and shout a single word. *"Kill."*

An owl appeared from his wristband, wings

spread wide and talons grasping for prey as it flew straight at Gessar's face with a screech to wake the dead.

Gessar's yelp of fear was almost drowned out, and he dropped me to fend off the attacking bird. His arms passed through the hologram without effect, and the owl's talons struck his eyes. They had no force behind them, but that didn't stop Gessar screaming and diving away in an uncoordinated dodge that took him off the throne's dais and into the ranks of his bodyguards, scattering them.

Tzaron lunged forward, taking advantage of the chaos, and pushed through the paralyzed line of defenders as I struggled to my feet. Our eyes met for a beautiful frozen moment and it felt like I saw into his very soul. Saw the conflict there, the desire to come to my aid against his need to kill Gessar and end the fight. I gave him the smallest of nods and knew he understood. If I'd used words, it would have been something like *'go fuck him up,'* but we didn't need words now.

Time resumed as Tzaron turned, snarling and brandishing what looked like a broken chunk of the pod's hull. Gessar made it to his feet, a wickedly sharp blade in one hand, the other raised high with claws ready to strike. The scattered guards tried to form up around their lord, their fear showing on their ssavs, abandoning a badly beaten Heshra. I gulped, trying to guess my chances of making it to the fallen laser rifle she still clung to. Not good, but better than Tzaron's odds against a half-dozen foes.

Before I could make my suicidal charge, Krosak slammed the butt of his spear on the floor.

"Fair duel challenge," he snapped at the guards. "Let the Sky Gods choose the best leader, it's not for us to interfere."

In unison, they raised their spears to point at the ceiling, stepping away from Gessar. The usurper's eyes widened — more in shock than in fear, I thought, though there was plenty of fear, too.

"Krosak, you wretch, get back here," he demanded as Tzaron stalked toward him. "I will carve your crimes on your bones for this, eater of dung!"

Krosak swallowed visibly but shook his head, and I saw his knuckles whiten on the haft of his spear. Though the tendrils of white and gray on his ssav showed his fear for all to see, he didn't move. Neither did his troops.

"One on one," Tzaron said, voice a low rumble

that seemed to shake the room. "No more hiding or threats. You will never threaten my taru-ma again."

And with that, he leaped. Gessar twisted to the side, slashing his wicked knife at Tzaron's throat. But my alien darling was no fool. Instead of attacking with his strange weapon, he used it to block Gessar's blade, swinging his tail out to stab with the deadly spine.

The exchange happened far quicker than it takes to describe it, and I barely followed what followed. In a blur of limbs, the two warriors came together cutting and hacking and stabbing, a lethal melee that I didn't want to watch but couldn't look away from. Gessar was bigger and stronger than Tzaron and he'd eaten a lot better these last few days. What if he won?

Then I get to find out if I can overload the gravity generators, I told myself. A messy, painful kill, one that would crush everyone in the palace under their own weight. I'd die too, but I'd have my revenge on Gessar. Without Tzaron, what else was there to hope for.

I kept edging toward the throne as the pair separated, bleeding and panting. Gessar sported a brand-new cut across his chest, Tzaron favored his left leg, but neither was injured enough to concede.

"Whoever slays this Zrin will be the new head of my guard," Gessar shouted, and I winced. That was an offer someone might listen to, and anyone joining Gessar in the fight might swing it — Tzaron was skilled, determined, and strong, but he was also exhausted and injured. Against weight of numbers, he might fail.

Might die.

And I wouldn't allow that. I just didn't have any idea what I'd do about it yet.

Krosak held firm, perhaps because it was his position being used as a bribe, and his hissed insistence kept the others from leaping to Gessar's defense. I saw the looks passed around, though, and knew with a bone-deep certainty that it wouldn't take long before one of them tried for the prize and that would be like a dam breaking.

It did, however, give me a chance to get closer to the throne. Flanking it, caged and restless, Sorcha and Kyrix whined. Close enough to get a good look at them, I shuddered at the sight of the mighty tengers reduced to this state. Ribs visible, skin sagging, they were a fraction of their former selves. Their great, sad eyes stared up at me, and I couldn't decide whether they were asking for my help or plotting to eat me. Maybe both.

One more reason for Tzaron to seek revenge. He loved his psychotic monster-pets and seeing them mistreated like this? If Gessar had killed them it would have been horrible but made sense. Leaving them here to starve as a public spectacle? *I saw red over that, and I barely knew them.*

23

TZARON

*M*y lungs burned, the long cuts where Gessar's claws had torn open my leg flooded my nerves with agony every time I took a step, and my energy reserves were draining far too fast.

None of that took the hungry grin from my face. I felt alive again after so long stuck in a tomb, as though I'd risen from the dead, and feeling pain only made that stronger. Gessar eyed my smile and backed away, knuckles white on the grip of his blade. This was far too much like a fair fight for him, especially when his guards weren't willing to face me for him.

I hadn't expected Krosak to put up a fight against the usurper, let alone for the guards to follow him, but he surprised me. So did they — none of the guards leaped at Gessar's order, whether out of disciplined obedience to Krosak or fear of me. It surprised Gessar too, distracting him for a heartbeat as he glared Krosak's way. I took advantage of that to pounce back into the fray, injured leg be damned.

My heavy, improvised ax moved like an extension of my arm, gliding through the air as though the Sky Gods had ordained a path for it to follow into Gessar's throat. For such a big Zrin, he was *fast,* but not fast enough to avoid a nasty cut to the face as he retreated. The weapon's ragged edge bit deep into his cheek, tearing through skin and the muscle below. Win or lose, I'd given him a scar to remember this fight by.

Gessar wasn't the kind of coward who fears pain, though, and the injury didn't faze him. My second attack met his dagger while he swung at me with claws and tail, forcing me back before I could take advantage of his wound. We were evenly matched — both of us experienced veterans of a thousand fights, my unorthodox ax making up for his size and reach. But if it came to an endurance contest, he had an edge, so I refused to let him wear me out.

My one advantage was Vicky-ma. Gessar fought a selfish battle, but I had a higher goal — I had my mate to defend, and that gave me the strength to ignore the aching tiredness pulling at my muscles, to stop retreating and step into Gessar's advance. Ducking under his knife cut, I saw his tail swing around to show what happened when you got too close to your opponent.

A good, solid move, but also predictable. My ax met Gessar's tail with a harsh crunch and the tip went limp, slapping my side rather than stabbing me with the deadly spine. One weapon out of Gessar's armory.

I tried to turn the ax back for a disemboweling strike but Gessar was too canny for that, and he knew the same tricks I did. Instead of withdrawing, he kept coming, slamming into me and knocking the air from my lungs. The impact would have sent me flying if not for his arms closing around me, wrapping me in a crushing embrace and pinning my arms to my side.

Claws dug into my back, my ribs creaked, and I couldn't breathe, so I did the only thing left to me — I attacked. Sinking my teeth into Gessar's shoulder, I clamped down hard as I could and shook my head, tearing at his flesh. His roar of anger and pain was the finest music I'd ever heard, and he threw me away with all his strength. I hit the floor hard, rolling to absorb the impact, tumbled into the line of guards surrounding our duel.

And one of them stabbed down at me. I'd given him the excuse he needed to kill me and claim the prize Gessar offered, and Krosak's orders wouldn't hold him back. My parry came almost too late, the spearhead carving a gash in my neck as I knocked it aside. Before he could pull back for another thrust, I sliced his stomach open with my tailspine and rolled away. The damage was done, though — he'd broken what control Krosak had over his cohort. They closed in around me, barely letting me get to my feet, and against a half dozen spears all the skill in the world wouldn't keep me from getting slaughtered. All it would do was delay the inevitable, and maybe take a few of them to the grave with me.

Krosak dithered behind his troops, as loyal as I could hope and as frightened as I feared. Gessar, meanwhile, roared in triumph and relief. The fight might not have been over yet, but he knew he'd won.

No, he hasn't, I told myself, measuring distance as I blocked and circled. None of the guards wanted to be the first to rush me — dying for a promotion had little value, so they'd fight with caution and wait for an opening.

That gave me time to maneuver, getting closer to

Gessar. Just a few more steps and I'd be in striking range of the usurper. Turning my back on the guards would mean my death, but I'd take Gessar by surprise and deal him what I hoped would be a fatal blow.

I'm sorry, Vicky-ma. I hoped I'd get to take you back to your home myself. You'll have to find your own way.

I braced myself to charge.

—and froze at the sound of a piercing whistle from the throne. Years of training and practice had set my fighting skills into my muscles, and my body kept blocking spear thrusts even as my attention focused on Vicky. She stood on the throne itself, glaring down like an avenging goddess. Even Gessar turned to look at her, giving me a perfect shot at his back. An opening I didn't take, too enthralled by my mate's display.

She stood tall and proud, throwing her arm out to point at the gang of guards surrounding me, and shouted a single word in my native tongue. Her pronunciation was terrible, but despite that her command was clear.

"*Eat!*"

And hot on the heels of that word came Sorcha and Kyrix, exploding forth from their cages in blinding-fast bursts of speed. Gessar screamed and jumped away, his ssav going white with fear, but he needn't have worried. Victoria hadn't aimed them at him.

Kyrix reached the guards first, her tentacles embracing one and pulling him down, a swipe of a paw knocking another flying, her claws opening him from groin to throat. Sorcha was just behind her sister, and less precise in her attack. She barreled through the crowd of guards, knocking them in every direction, tentacles and claws striking whoever she could reach.

The beautiful chaos they brought with them freed me to charge Gessar, and he spun to meet me, his outstretched knife forcing me to slow and circle. A desperate hope glittered in his eyes — I'd taken more than one spear wound, and loss of blood weighed my limbs down as though someone had tied rocks to my arms and legs. There wasn't very much left in me, and I lacked the strength to hide that. But still I came for him.

"Offer is still open, Tzaron," Gessar told me. "Surrender now and you and your human can go free."

I managed a half-grin, half-snarl at that. "Counteroffer: surrender now and I'll make your death painless and bury you with honor."

Sky Gods alone knew what my ssav looked like, but Gessar's was a winding mess of white, amber and red. Despite my condition, he wasn't confident of victory. To see him stripped of his confidence was a victory already.

But it wasn't enough for me.

Gessar circled with me, his knife dancing in the space between us, the constant motion making it hard to predict. His strategy was clear as fresh water. He didn't expect me to surrender, he intended to wait for me to fall from blood loss, then slit my throat. The longer I talked, the closer that moment came.

"Fuck you, Gessar," I said, using the insult as Vicky-ma had rendered into Sky Tongue as I stepped forward. It confused him as much as it had me, slowing his reflexes just enough to let me close.

I swung overhand at him as he thrust a moment too late. There wasn't anything wrong with his knife skills and the blade bit deep under my ribs. A wound that would finish the fight quickly and fatally.

But not instantly.

All my focus on my weapon, I ignored the wound and smashed my ax into his skull.

His roar of pain and fear gave me life, and I

struck again. Gessar tried pull his blade out of my torso to defend himself, but I grabbed hold of his wrist and held him tight. With his blade trapped inside me, he had no way to defend himself and I rained blow after blow on his head as the world faded around me.

24

VICTORIA

*T*he entire room went still as Tzaron buried his ax in Gessar's head. Letting go of the usurper, Tzaron held up his bloody hands and roared.

Gessar's body hit the deck and a wave of relief flooded through me. With it came the pain I'd been ignoring, the wound on my throat stinging, my limbs shaking, bruises all over me making themselves known. I didn't care.

We'd won. What else mattered?

Tzaron made his way toward the throne, and I jumped down to let him take it. Beside me, Heshra pulled herself to her feet, battered and bloody and smiling like a cat who'd done some *really impressive* mischief. In a way she had — she still held Gessar's laser rifle, a reminder of how much she'd contributed to our victory. As I stepped down from the throne, I took it from her with a nod of thanks.

Tzaron sat heavily, a murmur going around the crowd. Some sounded sympathetic, other greedy — no one missed how injured he was and how weak his wounds left him. My heart ached at the thought of how much he'd suffered to save me from Gessar, and now the vultures circled to pick the meat from his bones.

The voices quickly grew from whispers to shouts, Zrin roaring and squaring off against each other again. Bodies littered the room, and everyone had reason to be on edge, but from what little I understood of the shouting they were bickering over the horde's holdings. Would one of them inherit leadership from Tzaron? Or would they go their separate ways, and if so, how should the loot be divided up?

Tzaron's soft chuckle brought my attention back to him. "Victoria-ma, you are well named. Celebrate your win but go quickly. Heshra will see you home safely."

"Fuck you, Tzaron," I said, glancing at Heshra, who nodded and folded her arms. "We didn't go to all this trouble to give up on you."

"I know," he said, reaching up to stroke my cheek. Only when he touched my tears did I realize I was crying. "And I did not intend for this to be our last meeting. Alas, we do not get to choose the day of our deaths, only how we face it — and if I die saving you, then I've died as well as any Zrin."

My vision blurred by tears, I could barely see his infuriating roguish smile. I wanted so badly to say something witty, something romantic, but my mind chased itself in circles and all I felt was a tremendous loss.

"Fuck you, asshole," I muttered through the sobs, my chest tight. "You don't just get to die well and leave me alone."

The Zrins' ssavs made sense to me now as emotions fought over my mind and soul like tentacles trying to throttle each other. Joy at our victory, anger at what it cost, fear of what was to come, and all overwhelmed by a sense of loss that would break me if I let it.

I would not let it. Instead I focused on the anger, the unfairness of it all, and refused to accept this ending.

Leaning forward, I planted a kiss on his cheek. "I love you, Tzaron-ma, and I'm sorry."

Tzaron gave that a weary chuckle and started to

ask what I was apologizing for, but I didn't have time to listen. Straightening up, I turned and plucked the laser rifle from Heshra's startled hands.

If the crack of superheated air and the bright line of red light didn't draw everyone's attention, the shower of sparks as the beam cut into the ceiling certainly did. Dead silence fell as the Zrin stopped their bickering and turned to face me.

I admit, I hadn't really thought past this point, but I had their attention. Not wanting to waste that, I let my anger take the reins and go where it will.

"Are you all *mad,* or are you just too stupid to be trusted with sharp objects?" My voice came out raw and full of pain, reverberating through the room. The part of me that still reasoned realized that Count Catula had hooked into me into the speakers and cranked up the volume.

"Look at what following Tzaron-ma brought you, and how much you lost from Gessar's usurpation. Now you're talking about how to divide the flesh from a beast that shits gold. The horde can be your future, your legacy, a force to keep you — *all of you* — safe. Or it can be a distant memory in a decade, once all the treasure's spent and you're huddled in feuding groups again. Are you that fucking dumb?"

The whole assembly looked as if I'd slapped

them across the face with a dead fish, and I knew that if I paused, I'd lose my nerve. Or maybe come to my senses. Either way I'd stop antagonizing a room full of barbarian warriors, any of whom would slaughter me in a fair fight.

"You have a chance here to be part of something greater, but you'll tear it apart just because you don't like being in any group you're not in charge of. Tzaron knows that, Tzaron respects that, and Tzaron will give you the freedom to be yourselves. You've seen that, seen the effort he goes to welcoming each clan that joins the horde. Be the leaders your followers think you are and join him."

My shouted diatribe ran down there, leaving me panting and glaring at the crowd. One Zrin stepped forward, face hidden under a ceremonial helmet covered in feathers and fur.

"Tzaron is dead," he said roughly, his Sky Tongue cold and harsh. "What's left but to take what we can for—"

The laser rifle cracked again, crimson light carving through the ridiculous helmet and sending it flying. The Zrin froze in place, mouth dropping open in shock, and I lowered the rifle a fraction to aim for his chest.

I'd never have made that shot on purpose, not in

a million years. That shot had been intended as a warning, fired over his head not through his helmet. But the Zrin didn't need to know that.

Around him, other Zrin tensed, caught between the urge to rush me and wariness of my rifle. The moment one of them went for me it was all over. Before I could think a way to defuse the stalemate, twin roars sounded on either side of me as the tengers leaped forward to lash their tentacles and snarl. Between them, Count Catula added his tiny-but-ferocious roar to the sound, though I doubted it would dissuade anyone who ignored Sorcha and Kyrix's challenge.

In the frozen silent moment that followed, Heshra stepped up beside me, leaning on a spear. Savagely beaten, she still grinned with an unnerving intensity as she looked out into the crowd.

"Do what you like," she said. "But know that if you attack Tzaron's horde, I and my scouts stand with him."

As if by magic, the rest of the scouts appeared around us. The Zrin leaders' desire for a fight leached away visibly, looking at the odds. Not that we'd win, but we'd inflict casualties, and no one wanted to be weakened ahead of the civil war they all expected.

Krosak was next, though he stayed safely at the back. "We can war among ourselves, or we can follow Lord Tzaron to greater victories. My warriors stand with him."

That broke the dam, and other clan leaders started to shout their approval of Tzaron's leadership. Not all, but enough. Those who dissented did so quietly until one Zrin, standing safely at the back of the group, shouted the obvious objection.

"Skyless Depths, what use is this? Even if the human is right, even then, Tzaron's rule dies with him, and he will die within the day. We all see his wounds."

"What the *fuck* does that have to do with anything?" I snapped. "Haven't you heard? I am a witch. If I say Tzaron will live, trust me, he'll live. And if I'm wrong, you can have your fucking civil war once he's dead. Until then, be smart, be loyal, and *get Zsatia now*."

They stared at me, at us, and the future hung in the balance. The majority sided with Tzaron and me, yes, but all it would take was one Zrin deciding to take a chance. This fragile success teetered on the edge of a cliff, and a tiny push would send it down to shatter.

I searched for something more to say and came up empty.

"Those who do not listen to Victoria-ma are all fools, and none of you will lead this horde into anything other than civil war," Tzaron's rough voice boomed like thunder, filling the room with a force that threatened to knock me to the floor. Looking over my shoulder, my blood froze as I watched him pull himself to his feet, hiding the pain of moving from everyone but me.

Heshra made space for him beside me, and my alien mate put one arm around my shoulders as he glared out into the crowd. I forced myself not to wince as he leaned his weight on me — no one else needed to know how injured he was.

"My mate has told you nothing but the truth," he snarled, "yet still you are concerned with stripping the carcass of my horde before I am dead. Bury me before you divide my inheritance, or you are but ghouls feasting on your own futures and you will face my wrath."

The silent Zrin looked chastened, their ssavs writhing with embarrassment. Some looked at the floor, some at the ceiling, but none wanted to meet his eyes or mine. More than one looked at Gessar's corpse. He'd counted Tzaron out and died regretting it. No matter how injured Tzaron looked now, none of them wanted to be another example of the cost of underestimating us.

One step forward, then two. We walked toward the door and the crowd melted out of our way.

25

TZARON

Once I was sure no one but my allies would see, I allowed myself to slump against the cool wall of the corridor, groaning and fighting the pain. Vicky-ma whimpered as I took my weight off her, and I frowned.

"I am sorry, my love."

She gave me a look that, from anyone else, might have started a fight. "Tzaron-ma, what the hell do you think you have to apologize for? Lean on me all you like, idiot, I love you."

I opened my mouth, closed it with a snap. I had no desire to argue with those last three words.

"I love you as well," I said instead, pushing off the wall to stagger down the hall a little before leaning on the wall again. Groggily I realized I was leaving a blood trail, and that the world looked grayer than I remembered. Heshra supported me on my right, Vicky-ma on my left, and together we stumbled into Zsatia's chambers.

"Sweet Sunless Sky," she swore as I crashed against the shelving for support. Jars of herbs and pastes went flying, some smashing and filling the air with otherworldly fragrances. "What in the darkest cave have you done? You should be dead with wounds like that."

I managed a tired chuckle as Vicky pulled me towards the miraculous sarcophagus. "So they keep telling me, Zsatia, but my taru-ma is too stubborn to accept that."

"Damned straight," Vicky-ma muttered at that, pulling the cover of the strange machine open. "I've been through too much to find you, and I'm not losing you now."

Before I managed a reply, she pushed me toward the fog-filled interior. Even in my weakened condition, she lacked the strength to move me, but I took the hint and rolled back into the chamber.

The fog felt strange, cold but not unpleasant. My burden of pain became easier to carry, didn't bother me at all, though I knew the injuries were still there. The door closed over me, and then there was nothing but the cool grip of the fog. I lay back, content to let my mate's magic heal me before I saw her again.

THE DOOR OPENED ABOVE ME, and I realized I had no idea how much time had passed. It might be hours, it might be days, for all I knew years might have passed while I lay there, letting human magic heal my fatal wounds.

I didn't care, so long as Vicky-ma was still there. Just the thought of seeing her sent a wave of joyful energy washing through me, and I almost bounced to my feet to see the medbay in chaos. Every bed full, a Zrin waiting in every chair, Zsatia rushing from injury to injury, trying to heal as well as keep order.

"Thank the Endless Sky you're out of there," she said, her vehement reaction surprising me. Perhaps the healer considered me a friend, despite her gruff demeanor? "You've been hogging the miracle box for hours, and I've got too many patients who need it. Out!"

Or perhaps not, though I thought I heard some fondness in her harsh voice. Laughing, I leaped over the side of the box. I felt like I could fight the world, but I had more important things to deal with than violence.

"Where is Vicky-ma?"

"Am I your personal assistant to keep track of your mate for you?" Zsatia snapped back as she lifted a half-dead Zrin and carried him towards the miraculous healing machine I'd just vacated. "Haven't you given me enough work already?"

Arguing would be fruitless and disrespectful, so I nodded and thanked her for her work before leaving to seek Victoria. The Zrin I passed saluted, fist to chest, acknowledging my rule, and giving me plenty of space. It took a moment for me to realize why — the human magic had cleaned the blood from my limbs but not from my clothes. And by now the word of my duel with Gessar would have spread, growing in the telling.

Now here I was, unmarked by injury yet covered in blood. No wonder my followers were awestruck. They'd get over it — Zrin warriors weren't so easily cowed — but in the meantime they saw me as a figure out of legend.

Though they were eager to serve, no one knew where I could find Vicky-ma. I ground my teeth at the third lack of an answer. How could no one have seen where my mate went? She was the only human in the palace, the only human for days of travel, yet no one saw where she'd gone.

It took me entirely too long to work out what that meant. I had shown her the perfect hiding place, and my Vicky-ma would want to be away from Zrin in case of more treachery. Taking the stairs three at a time, I rushed up and into the forbidden area. Before Vicky's arrival they'd been dangerous. Mapping my way through this tangled mess had taken days of dedicated work, the complete darkness an invitation to step in a gap or impale myself on shards of torn metal. Some said the dead hunted in these shadows, creeping up on the unaware. Now, dim lighting flickered overhead, making it easy to bypass those dangers.

"Vicky-ma," I called out, my voice echoing. No response. Had I guessed wrong?

Having no idea where else I might find her, I pressed on. The ghostly light from the ceiling cast eerie shadows in the curving corridor, and in some ways it was even creepier than it had been in the dark. Safer, yes, but the eerie shadows had a haunted look. Screech made frightened little hooting noises. Rather than flying ahead, he sat on my forearm, huddled into me.

"Shush," I told him with a smile. "You weren't

frightened when I sent you into battle. What ruffles your feathers now?"

He didn't reply, just turned his head to look up at me with a withering glare. I put words to that look easily enough: *"Of course Gessar didn't scare me, I'm a hologram. But ghosts? Who knows what they can hurt?"*

I chuckled, acknowledging the point. Ahead of us a doorway came into view, light shining out of it. Had I reached it already? Even ghostly light made the journey so much easier.

Stepping into the doorway, my heart caught. There Victoria sat, cross-legged and chewing on one lip as she concentrated on the obsidian god-cube. Beside her, the spectral form of her spirit companion lay stretched out, and above him hung intangible tablets full of writing that changed as I watched.

I looked on in silence, not wanting to disturb my beloved. Too intent on her work to notice my arrival, she leaned in to draw on the stone with her finger, the fiery lines within moving to follow her gesture until at last an image formed in the flames, circles within circles all around a central orb. And on each circle hung another orb, each circling the center. Some of those had further orbs of their own, moving in a complex dance.

Simple but beautiful, the display hung inside the

obsidian block and Vicky stretched, drawing my attention from the art she'd created. Something gave me away, some sound I made or maybe the feel of me watching, and Vicky looked around at me without the shock I expected. Her face, already more beautiful than any work of art, blossomed into a smile that by rights should have lit up the room.

"You could have left word of where to find you," I said, breaking the silence and cursing myself for the accusatory tone my words took.

But Vicky only laughed, blue eyes sparkling. "Of course I could, but who to trust? That's why I wanted to get out of sight of your people after all: any of them might have tried holding me prisoner to make you cooperate."

"I'd kill anyone who tried," I told her. "If they hurt you, I'd kill them slowly."

She laughed, a musical sound. "I know, Tzaron-ma, I know. But none of us knew how long you'd be healing for — someone might be crazy enough to try it. There's been enough death in our horde, don't you think?"

Our horde? My breath caught and my heart nearly burst with joy and pride when she said that. Even so, I crouched before her and spoke, low and serious. There were limits I did not want to push her past, I'd discovered. Here, she was alone, surrounded by enemies and without a single member of her own species to turn to. I couldn't force that life on her, no matter how much I wanted her to stay.

"You do not have to stay if you do not wish it, Vicky-ma. I will return you safely to your home if you ask, and that need not be the end of our relationship unless you want it to."

Her reaction took me by surprise, a punch that landed her fist square on my jaw. The impact rocked my head back and made her yelp, shaking her hand and swearing under her breath.

"If you're going to hit me, at least let me teach you how to throw a punch and where to aim it," I chided her, struggling to keep from laughing.

"If you don't like how I punch, don't insult me like that," Vicky retorted, failing to hide her grin. "This is home now. *You* are my home."

Tension I hadn't noticed drained from my muscles, and I let out a sigh of relief. "I hoped you'd say that, my love. But we can still visit your people, when you like."

"We can do more than that, I think," she said, her brow creasing. "I'm sure our people can help each other out..."

She trailed off into thoughtful silence and I

watched, smiling. It only took a moment for her to shake herself free of whatever idea briefly stole her attention. "We can talk about that later, though. Here, look, I've solved one puzzle in your 'god-cube' and I think I've got a handle on another couple."

She turned to point out what she'd done, but I caught her chin and turned her back to face me. "I believe we have more important matters to address first, my love."

She gasped, eyes widening as I leaned in to kiss her. Her lips hot against mine, she moaned, and if her racing pulse hadn't betrayed her eagerness, the tremor that went through her before she pulled back did.

"Aren't you forgetting something?" she asked, flushed and grinning. I growled. Her blush deepened at that, and she struggled to look at me as she continued. "You, um, promised to punish me if I put myself in danger again."

"Threatened," I corrected her. "I threatened to punish you."

A tiny grin and a shrug told me she didn't see it that way.

26

VICTORIA

Now why the hell did I remind him of that? I looked up into his eyes, the strange golden flecks dancing as he watched my blush spread. My pulse almost deafened me as his finger ran across my cheek, claw extended just enough to scratch rather than wound.

Tzaron's deep, dark chuckle sent a tremor through me, and I bit my lip, trying to hold back a moan. A futile effort. There was no hiding how aroused I was, how badly I needed my man, how much I wanted him to take me.

"It's true, you were disobedient," Tzaron said, trailing his claw down my neck. "I value my mate above my life, and you risked yourself to save me."

"In my defense, I wouldn't have lasted long

without you here," I said. Now that he'd taken my suggestion, I wasn't at all sure I wanted to find out what he had in mind for me.

No, that wasn't true. The idea frightened me, but not like the battle had. More like the feeling when the roller coaster starts to move, and you realize you're committed to it. Whatever drops and loops and twists were ahead, I'd signed on willingly.

Still, my nerves made me try to pull away as Tzaron's claw scraped across my skin, and he chuckled. With a single, sweeping motion, he sliced through the t shirt and the bra beneath it, exposing my breasts.

I stepped back clutching the clean-cut edges of my clothes, staring at him and mouthing words without speaking them. His grin spread, sharp teeth on display as he followed me, hands moving lightning fast. In moments my clothes were in shreds, torn away to leave me naked and panting for breath.

His deadly claws hadn't left a scratch on me.

The shiver that ran through me wasn't from the chilly air.

"Come here," Tzaron said, and though he spoke calmly, kindly even, it wasn't a request. It was an order, and I obeyed without thinking, stepping back into his grasp. His strong hands closed around my upper arms, lifted me to him, his grip just barely short of hurting me as he kissed my neck, razor-sharp teeth dragging across my skin. I couldn't help myself. Letting out a whimper, I twisted in his grip, trying to hold him, to pull my naked body against him.

"Oh no you don't," Tzaron said, pushing me back again. "I know your ways, little one, and if I let you, you'll keep me distracted from punishing you."

"I'm not—" he cut my protests short with a glare, and I had to admit he was right. I might not have consciously been trying to keep him focused on something else, but my subconscious had other ideas.

Though he wasn't helping himself by stripping me naked.

"You know better than to argue, Vicky-ma," Tzaron's voice was low, almost a whisper.

With a quick, rough motion, Tzaron spun me around and bent me over the stone altar beside the god-cube. Just minutes ago, the puzzles in the stone were all I could think about, but now they were nothing, a distraction. All that mattered was *him*, Tzaron, my mate. Pressed against the cold stone, I whimpered and spread my legs without needing to be told. Tzaron chuckled again, his breath against my ear as he unbuttoned his leather kilt and let it fall to the floor.

"You need to learn to look after yourself," he said. "I need you alive and well, and I will not tolerate you risking your life for mine."

"I saved you," I protested. "You needed me."

Tzaron's answer was to smack me across my ass, a single, solitary spank that echoed off the walls. My indignant yelp followed close behind as the stinging impact rushed through me.

"Irrelevant," he whispered in my ear. "You put yourself in danger, and I will not tolerate that. Your survival, your wellbeing, these things matter more than my life."

Another firm, stinging smack, making me squirm in his grip. The stinging hurt, yes, but it was also deeply, deeply erotic, and I bit my lip to keep from moaning. Tzaron didn't need to know about the effect he was having on me.

"You will stay safe, Victoria-ma. Or I will teach you to do so."

The third smack made me gasp and moan, tingling all over. *Was that supposed to discourage me? Because right now it's having the opposite effect.* I had the presence of mind not to say it out loud and tempt him to make the punishment harder.

Or, worse still, to stop it altogether.

"Yeah, well, I feel the same about you," I told him instead. "Are *you* going to give up dangerous missions because I worry?"

Not the best of responses, but I wasn't thinking straight. My blood burned with shock and pain and love and excitement, and it was like thinking through cotton wool. Tzaron's hand came down again, leaving my behind burning and my heart pounding.

This time he kept his hand on me, squeezing and stroking, teasing. Rough fingers pressing into my tender skin, not painfully, but with an unmistakable intent to claim me.

And, oh boy, did I want him to claim me.

"This is not a matter for debate," my alien tyrant said. "I will not have you endangering yourself. You will behave, you will take care of yourself, and you will leave the battles to me."

As he finished, he bit my shoulder, just hard enough to make me squeal and shudder. Bent over me, his body rested against mine, and his dick felt like a rod of iron pressed against me. A reminder of how big he was, and again I wondered how that would ever fit inside me.

I wanted to find out more than anything.

"Are you doing this because it'll teach me a lesson?" I asked, twisting to try to look him in the face. "I think maybe you're doing it because you enjoy it."

Pressed against my back, Tzaron chuckled. The vibration moved through me, and he stroked down between my legs, a finger gliding across my pussy lips and coming away wet with my juices. "I'm not the only one, my mate."

I started to protest, only to be silenced as he pressed that finger inside me. Whatever words I'd meant to say turning into a low, uncontrolled moan, an undeniably desperate sound.

Yes, it said, I wanted him. Needed him. I wriggled, pushing back against him, and Tzaron laughed a low, dark, so-fucking-sexy laugh. "Fuck you," I protested.

"Yes. That is the idea."

His lips brushed mine and my body responded before my mind had even registered the touch. Restrained as I was, I still pushed myself toward him, kissing back hard as his long, flexible tongue probed my mouth.

Cock hardening even further, Tzaron growled into the kiss and pulled my legs aside roughly. My breath caught as his huge, hard, rough dick pressed against my wet pussy, sliding into position as he withdrew his finger.

And paused there. Tempting, teasing, making me desperate and eager to do whatever he wanted if only he'd fuck me.

"Are you going to be good, my little one?" Tzaron whispered, and oh god that tone. Dark and powerful, it was impossible to ignore or refuse.

I tried, tried so hard, to say no. What came out of my lips was a croaked, "Yes."

A surrender, and a final one. Tzaron was irresistible, everything about him turned me on. His smile, his strength, the texture of his skin. The powerful, masculine scent of him, and *oh god* his cock.

And most of all, the strength of his devotion to me.

His thrust managed to take me by surprise, even though I'd been waiting for it. He growled as he buried himself inside me, his marvelous cock driving deep into me, spreading and stretching me. It was almost painful and entirely wonderful.

I pushed back against him, eager, hungry for more. Tzaron growled at that, fucking me harder, deeper, every thrust pushing me down against the altar, pinning me there. The contrast between his warmth and the cool stone beneath me added to the waves of sensation that washed through me.

Scraping his claws down my back, Tzaron increased the pace, fucking me ever harder, ever faster, until I thought I'd explode from the pent-up pleasure rocking my body. My world shrank, everything else fading away into a fog of ecstasy. All that mattered was Tzaron and what he did to me.

His tail slid gently, dexterously, across my pussy — a contrast to the rough, powerful pounding of his cock. But when he found my clit, oh my god, it sent an explosion rippling along my nerves, every muscle tensing and shaking, leaving my body shaking and bucking.

Somewhere in there, I realized I was screaming, howling with joy as he fucked me into oblivion. Everything went white, and for a moment I thought I must have died and gone to heaven. Angels sang, light was all around, and my body shook with orgasm after orgasm before I eventually came to my senses, still draped across the stone altar, Tzaron behind me. A shiver ran through him as I rolled over onto my back and looked up at him.

"What gives?" I asked, panting the words as I struggled for air. "I thought you were going to punish me."

Tzaron laughed, a full-bodied roar of good humor that shook the room and left me smiling. "That was the plan, Vicky-ma, but you are just so damned distracting."

"We'll just have to try again, then," I said. *And again, and again, until the stars go out.*

27

EPILOGUE

*N*ight fell and the horde gathered, watching silently as I descended the ramp at Tzaron's side. Under the hot Crashland sun, the New City was almost unbearable during the summer day, but in the drowsy warmth of twilight it came alive.

What a difference a year made. What had once been a temporary camp had become a permanent settlement, and the horde hosted guests from a dozen other states. Not all Zrin, either — the Vale representatives looked ill at ease, but they'd insisted on being here.

Clans still fought each other. The work of turning the ragtag gathering of outlaws into a cohesive empire would take years, but Tzaron's swift justice had taken hold. Traders could visit without fear of being robbed now, and the wealth the Zrin horde took in plunder brought merchants from half the planet.

The biggest change, though, gurgled in my arms. Little Jezka — a compromise name, I'd wanted to call our daughter Jessica and Tzaron had wanted to call her something he could pronounce — wriggled delightedly as Count Catula played with her. It never seemed to faze Jezka that the cat wasn't there when she grabbed him, and it didn't keep her from trying to catch the elusive hologram.

"She has your enthusiasm," Tzaron said, slipping his arm around my shoulders and holding me as we left the ramp and entered the city.

"And your appetite," I mock-complained to Tzaron's amusement. "Our little imp will eat the world if we aren't careful."

"Good. She needs to eat if she's to grow into the mighty warrior she's destined to be."

"Oh no, no thank you. Bad enough worrying about *you* on a raid, I'm not letting you drag Jezka along too!"

"We'll see," Tzaron said, smiling, and I knew I'd lost the debate. If Jezka wanted to be a warrior, she would be. And I knew she'd be good at the job if she chose it.

The crowd closed around us as we walked, eager to see the baby. The *royal* baby, I thought. A year on and it still hadn't entirely sunk in. My daughter was Princess Jezka Bern, heir to the horde and proof that humans and Zrin could breed. We'd have to guard her privacy carefully if she was going to have any hope of a normal life.

I almost laughed at the thought as her tail escaped and wrapped around my wrist. A normal life didn't seem to be in the cards for my little one.

Zrin stepped out of our way, calling out congratulations. A few dared try to touch Jezka or me, only to be warned off by Tzaron's snarl. I'd argued for guards lining our route, but Tzaron refused to appear fearful of his own people. My mate was too brave sometimes — only a year since Gessar tried to overthrow him, and he insisted he needed no protection from his people.

It was a beautiful sentiment, but it hadn't stopped me having a word with Heshra. Her scouts blended into the crowd, ready to pounce on any would-be assassins. With both my mate and my daughter out here, I wasn't going to take any chances.

Ahead of us the crowd parted, leaving space for us to approach the small altar erected at the center of the city. And on it, the god-cube waited, fires burning inside.

"You are sure you have this right, Vicky-ma?" Tzaron's effortless self-assurance failed him around the cube, and I didn't blame him. It held questions that no Zrin could answer simply because they lacked the technology, barely in humanity's grasp, and it had taken all year for me to solve it, even with access to the database.

"I'm certain," I said. "I wouldn't have agreed to this stunt otherwise."

I still didn't know if it was a good idea, but the symbolism was too tempting. The fire inside the cube marked a complex pattern, one that described Crashland's position in the galaxy. All done except the last piece, one line to be marked.

Tzaron took my hand, and together we took Jezka's, the three of us together completing that last link, solving the puzzle. All around us, the crowd waited in eager silence, waiting for the cube's reaction.

For a moment, nothing. Then a blinding pillar of light shot skyward. I flinched back, my eyes watering, and Tzaron raised a hand to shield himself from the blinding intensity. Jezka merely gurgled happily.

You might get to travel to the stars yourself, I thought. Whoever had planted these puzzles eons ago must be watching for the signal. Perhaps the Sky Gods of Zrin legend were on their way already?

Until they arrived, I had my family here, and that was all I'd need.

The End

Thank you for reading *Tied to the Alien Tyrant!* Please take a moment to leave an opinion about the book, I appreciate every review.

I'll return to Crashland with the Crashland Contact Romances! Check out my website or join my mailing list for more news!
If you'd like to hear more about my upcoming releases, sign up for my mailing list:
Leslie Chase newsletter

And if you're on Facebook, join Leslie's Legion to connect with me and your fellow readers!

CRASHLAND SAGA

Crashland Colony Romances

AURIC

Crashed on an unexplored planet, with only an alien warrior and a holographic cat for company... what's a girl to do?

TORRAN

Stranded on the wrong planet, captured by brutal alien raiders, the only good thing about Lisa's situation is Torran. He's a dangerous alien warrior - who also happens to be the hottest man she's ever met. Strong, protective, and lethal, he's everything she could want or need.

Perhaps she shouldn't have shot him on sight?

RONAN

Trapped with a sexy alien warrior, a holographic owl, and a mystery she needs to solve. Becca doesn't like the prytheen, she doesn't trust them, and she is absolutely not interested in this one.

So why is she having so much trouble keeping her hands off him?

Crashland Castaway Romances

ABOUT LESLIE CHASE

LESLIE CHASE

I love writing, and especially enjoy writing sexy science fiction and paranormal romances. It lets my imagination run free and my ideas come to life! When I'm not writing, I'm busy thinking about what to write next or researching it – yes, damn it, looking at castles and swords and spaceships counts as research.

If you enjoy my books, please let me know with a review. Reviews are really important and I appreciate every one. If you'd like to be kept up to date on my new releases, you can sign up for my email news-letter by **following this link** — subscribers get a free science fiction romance novella!

www.leslie-chase.com

ARE YOU A STARR HUNTRESS?

Do you love to read sci fi romance about strong, independent women and the sexy alien males who love them?

Starr Huntress is a coalition of the brightest Starrs in romance banding together to explore uncharted territories.

If you like your men horny- maybe literally- and you're equal opportunity skin color-because who doesn't love a guy with blue or green skin?- then join us as we dive into swashbuckling space adventure, timeless romance, and lush alien landscapes.

Sign up for our mailing list here: http://eepurl.com/b_NJyr

Dragons of Mars

The remains of the Dragon Empire have slumbered on Mars for a thousand years, but now the ancient shifters are awake, alive, and searching for their mates!

Each book can be read on its own, but you'll get the best effect if you read them in order.

- DRAGON PRINCE'S MATE
- DRAGON PIRATE'S PRIZE
- DRAGON GUARDIAN'S MATCH
- DRAGON LORD'S HOPE
- DRAGON WARRIOR'S HEART

Worldwalker Barbarians

Teleported from Earth to a far-off planet, found by blue skinned wolf-shifter aliens, and claimed as mates. Is this disaster or delight for the feisty human females?

1: Zovak

2: Davor

Silent Empire books

Romance in a Galactic Empire

Each of these books follows the story of a different woman, snatched from Earth and thrust into the Silent Empire — a galaxy-spanning nation of intrigue and romance. Read to see them find their alien mates amongst the stars.

Each of these books can be read as a standalone, though they share some characters.

- STOLEN FOR THE ALIEN PRINCE
- STOLEN BY THE ALIEN RAIDER
- STOLEN BY THE ALIEN GLADIATOR

The Alien Explorer's Love

Can Two Beings from Different Worlds Find Common Ground — And Love?

Jaranak is an alien explorer on a rescue mission to Earth, but now he's stranded here at the dawn of the 20th century. And his efforts to go unnoticed are bring thwarted by Lilly, a human female who won't stop asking questions. She should be insufferable, but instead he finds himself unable to get the sassy woman out of his mind...

Mated to the Alien Lord

a Celestial Mates novel by Leslie Chase

Love is never easy. Love on an alien world is downright dangerous!

With her life on Earth going nowhere, Gemma needs a fresh start. Enter the Celestial Mates Agency, who say they can match her with the perfect alien. And despite the dangers of his planet, Corvax is everything she could have asked for — impossibly hot, brave, and huge.

Now that she's seen him, there's no way she's going back.

Arcane Affairs Agency

A shared world of shifters, vampires, far, and witches - full of everything that goes bump in the night! Check out the full list of books **here**.

THE BEAR AND THE HEIR, by Leslie Chase

When Cole North arrives in Argent Falls to investigate reports of magical storms, he doesn't expect much to come of it. Not after the series of pointless missions the Arcane Affairs Agency has sent him on recently. This time, though, it's different. The small town is plagued by bizarre weather, the storms are trying to warn him off, and there are *fae* running wild. And then there's Fiona.

No matter how much the bear shifter tries to focus on his mission, he can't get the hot, curvy girl out of his head. But the fae are after her too – and when they try and kidnap her, Cole's mission and his feelings for Fiona collide.

Guardian Bears

Ex-military bear shifters providing protection from the threats no one else can deal with. Each book is a stand-alone plot, as the sexy bears find their curvy mates.

1. GUARDIAN BEARS: MARCUS
2. GUARDIAN BEARS: LUCAS
3. GUARDIAN BEARS: KARL

Tiger's Sword

A four-part paranormal romance serial about Maxwell Walters, billionaire tiger shifter, and his curvy mate Lenore.

Box Set, collecting all four parts

1. Tiger's Hunt
2. Tiger's Den
3. Tiger's Claws
4. Tiger's Heart

Printed in Great Britain
by Amazon

65275011R00220